For Jackie, Walkman and Mom and Dad

Special thanks to Pinky for all her help

THE JACKET PHOTO

One

As authors go, Keith Randall fell somewhere between J. D. Salinger and God. There were people who knew that he existed and there were people who believed that he existed, but one had only slightly more chance of meeting Keith than the other two. One person who knew of Keith was of his agent, Lannie Reyes. Lannie's secondary job was finding buyers for Keith's work. Her primary one was putting up with Keith. That one kept getting harder.

"Okay Keith, this new manuscript, or 'junk' as you call it, requires special attention? What am I missing here? Everything that you've done, you call me and I come. You give me an envelope, I go to the publisher. Publisher raves, we get paid. You stay here, I refill my Prozac. Why do you have to mess up what has worked perfectly for five years?"

"I don't want this under my name, Lannie. It's a romance, and Keith Randall does not write romances." was the gravelly reply. A handsome man in his mid thirties, Keith hadn't ventured from his cabin in a few years. Two addictions were the cause, and the main one ended the day his wife died. Crawling inside a bottle may not have been the rational response, but he was not one given to rational spurts. After pouring out the contents of his guts one too many times, he'd decided to start with the contents of his head. Once a computer and a fax machine had been delivered, he found a voice that could not be silenced. He wrote of dark people doing dark things, and even his heroes were scarred or flawed. Redemption always had to be worked for, and justice was swift and painful. On a lark, he called the first number that he saw in a literary magazine. Within two weeks, Lannie called him back. What followed was astounding. Three straight debuts at number one. Newspaper articles and magazines were trumpeting him as the next "Great American Author". Television producers wanted him for interviews. As he turned them all down, his reputation grew as a malcontent. He was called a "misanthrope", hating humanity while profiting from it. But the public kept buying the books, and Keith kept on writing.

"A romance?" Lannie asked, incredulously. "The poster boy for cynics found his heart?"

"Ha fucking ha, Lannie. This is the last book for that deal you had me sign with this publisher. It can be anything according to them, just as long as I write it."

"So... if not your name, then who?" Lannie asked. It was a fair question, considering that she would need this knowledge and more in order to get the publisher to bite. Fortunately, Keith had this question, plus the next few, already answered.

"Okay, I've been thinking about this for a while, and it's covered. Her name is 'Kaycee Landing', and here's a picture for you to use on the jacket. What do you think?"

"Well," Lannie began, "I'm glad it isn't you in drag. Who is she? And better yet, do you have permission to use this photo?"

"As for her real name, I don't know. You know how you go to the department store and all the frames already have pictures in them for display purposes? I found a frame in the attic and this was inside. I made a few calls and found the agency that had the rights to the photo. Their rep said that all of their photos were public domain, and therefore I could use the shot with no ifs, ands or buts."

"You have been busy, huh? All right bright boy, tell me this: why a woman?"

"It's obvious," said Keith. "Most romances are written by women, and read by women. Why mess with the natural order of things? Besides, I don't do tours or personal appearances, so no one gets screwed. We all get to be as happy as we can be. The publisher can quit swigging Pepto-Bismol, you can buy yourself some more shoes, and I get more money to use to completely cut myself off from humanity. It's a beautiful thing."

The self-satisfied look that Keith had on his face was making Lannie glad that she had blown off her three-martini lunch. It wasn't that Keith was a bad guy, but his wife's death had left him seemingly heartless, and it was unsettling to see him this way. Normally Keith's range went from gruff and depressed to morose and morbid, but today he had climbed all the way up to slightly personable. Lannie had to admit that the publisher would be happy, she'd get another big percentage and Keith would be able to keep sliding down his banister into oblivion.

"Okay Keith, I'll take it in. They'll love it and put the big promotional wheels behind it. We'll all make money and the world will love Kaycee Landing. However, I don't know how much more solitude you can take babe."

"I don't need anybody to make me feel… anything. Unlike some others."

"Bite me, Keith." and with that statement, Lannie was out the door.

Two

Keith stood up and stretched. Against his better judgment, he liked Lannie. Odd, he thought, since he hadn't been able to even tolerate any other human being after Mel died. Mel was his good side, the one that allowed him to function in the world. She was the only one that could see through the cocoon that he had woven about himself, the only one who had tried, really. His parents were dutiful enough to make sure that their only child entered into the world without a hitch, but within a few years, a constant hate seeped into their marriage, which ended the night of Keith's fifth birthday. As he grew, Keith learned how a person could get along without other people. His father, whom he saw only twice yearly, had effectively used his sales job to replace his friends. His mother just moved around the house in a slight state of madness, becoming more involved with the families she saw on television than in the life of her son. Following their examples of self-involvement, Keith threw himself into school. Naturally bright, and with a gifted imagination, he was an excellent student. No one realized that the reason that Keith was so proficient in his studies was that he simply didn't do anything else. A teacher asked him once, after Keith had delivered another impressive paper, why he wouldn't try out for the drama club or football. His answer was curt and simple: "I don't need any more people in my life."

Keith had already pre-enrolled at U of M when his graduation day came, and a week after he was already taking summer classes. On his way across the campus one afternoon, he slammed blindly into another student, knocking them both to the ground. As he regained his stance, he vaguely noticed that the other student's books and portfolio were scattered across the path. Not planning an apology or a helping hand, Keith turned on his heel and took a step away. No sooner had he moved than an incensed voice called after him.

"Randall you bastard! If you don't get back here and help me up, I swear to God that I'll kick your ever-loving ass!"

"Bastard? Kick my ass?" he muttered. Who was this woman, Keith thought, and where does she get off talking to me that way? He turned to face her, and saw that she was still sitting on the ground, books and papers still in disarray.

"You fully expect me to go over there and hoist you up, don't you?" Keith asked. The received reply was simply a sly grin and a look down her nose. "I can't believe that I'm doing this. Why should I help you?"

"Because you should, maybe…?" Again, she flashed that same smile and offered her hand, raised up to his. He grabbed it, intending to pull her upright forcefully, but after feeling her grip, he knew that this plan would not succeed. As she stood, she came within three inches of Keith's face. Keith jumped back, uncomfortable with someone violating his personal space. When his four feet of territory was re-established, he looked at this other student. She seemed vaguely familiar, and she was actually quite pretty. Her dark hair was shot with a mix of pink and blonde streaks, and she wore a tee shirt and boxer shorts, which Keith instantly recognized as the uniform of an art student. As she gathered her things, a glance at some sketches bore out that hypothesis.

"Good thing there isn't any wind today, or you'd be across campus trying to run that stuff to ground." Keith said.

"And I suppose that I wouldn't get any help with that either, huh? By the way, I'm Melanie Oliphant, but friends call me Mel. You can call me Mel, too Keith."

"There's that again. You're too familiar with me. I don't know you, and you presume to call me by name? And why are you looking behind me?"

"Your horse," Mel answered. "The high one that you fell off of when you ran me over. He's got to be around here somewhere..."

"Spare me, please, from the edge of your razor wit. I'm leaving now, *Melanie*."

"Keith, wait!" She yelled. "I'm sorry. Boy, you just cannot be razzed, can you? I'm in your Eastern Civics class. I sit behind you and daydream about what's on the front of the back of your head throughout the entire period. I'm glad I finally got to see your face. It's very nice, you know."

"Why me?" Keith wondered aloud. No one had noticed him socially before, but that was partly by design. Getting attention, especially from women, was something that would totally throw his entire life into a spin.

Just imagining it made him sweat, or perhaps that was the Melanie effect. He felt a bit queasy as he ran through all the perceived relationship pitfalls that he had stored away for these types of emergencies. Going to parties, dating, or eating in front of others, it all seemed like so much unnecessary torture. He had structured his life so that he didn't need his fellow human beings, and here was someone who seemed to want to upset that balance. Although it was somewhat against his will, he did help Mel pick up her books, and he did walk the rest of the way across campus with her. Something in the way that she had looked at him, and the subtle electricity that he felt when he grasped her hand confused him, and he found that he truly wanted to learn more about her. The next day, during a trek to class that they *had* planned, Mel would "accidentally" brush against him as they walked. That contact proved as absolutely addictive to him, and he was hooked.

Since meeting her, a crack had formed in his resolve, just wide enough for one person to get inside, and when Mel had gotten all the way in, Keith's shell had closed tightly, (but gently,) around her. Keith hadn't realized that he truly needed someone until the day that he had met Mel.

At first, like the starving man, he was greedy, ravenous for her attention and her time. She would tell him that she "couldn't be his life", but that she "could be part of it". Mel had her dreams, her friends and a family that she would not forsake for Keith, and he would have to accept those facts. Their first few dates were hardly monumental, taking place in either his apartment or her dorm, if her roommate was gone.

Being able to talk to someone that he respected was a wonderful feeling for Keith. He poured parts of himself out to Mel that he had held inside for so long. Things about his childhood, memories that he had buried for ages it seemed. She was a great listener, but wasn't afraid to tell Keith when; whether in the past or currently, he was being an insufferable ass. But it was so easy to talk to her. He would lose himself in her eyes, running and flying until he felt safe. She amazed him with the way that she viewed life.

She was a daredevil, always leaping from the highest rung, instinctively knowing that things were going to be okay no matter where she landed. Mel took Keith for a drive once, just "around the way", she had said. Keith nodded off in the passenger seat and woke up in Pennsylvania. He was instantly furious, but Mel could calm him like no other, and as she would have predicted, everything was okay – much to his chagrin.

Mel wanted to own a gallery; somewhere that would hold not only her paintings, but other so-called "starving artists" as well. Keith told her that such an idea wouldn't work, because there was no way that that type of artist could ever get up the ambition required to actually exhibit something. That remark had hurt her, and was the first time, even indirectly, that his boiling cynicism for the world had bubbled over and scalded her. He apologized; another first, and Mel accepted, but it took Keith two more weeks to get over his own words. He was sheepish around her, not wanting to rock the boat again for fear of losing her forever. Mel replied that she was "in for the long haul, and that arguments happen". Mel told him that she had always been attracted to mysterious men and a guy that never spoke or turned around in class was a mystery that would make Agatha Christie proud. That was the guy with whom she'd fell in love. That was the first time either of them had mentioned the word "love", but it didn't seem scary in the least. Rather, it served to release some pressures that both had been feeling. They quickly decided to get engaged, and Keith, as well as Mel, knew that they each had found their soul mate.

Married life amazed Keith. Mel had true talent, and her work was incredible. She thought that Keith would be a great agent for her, seeing as he really didn't care about anyone's feelings or stepping on anyone's toes. After throwing a mock defense at her for those comments, he agreed that he would try it. Soon, they both discovered that indeed, Keith was good at the agent game for those very reasons. That and a fierce love for a wife who deserved everything he could give to her.

Working on hunches, Keith was able to find the right galleries and the right crowds to effectively show off Mel's wonderful art. She was quickly becoming the toast of the Midwest's small but growing art scene, and it seemed as if everyone knew someone that had one of her paintings. Up late one night after a particularly lethal combination of fish burritos and stale beer, Keith woke Mel to offer proof of her star status; somebody had used one of her paintings as the prize in a terribly bad action film.

At times, Keith had to just stop to look around him. The man who had no use for anybody suddenly loved so much he ached. He couldn't imagine his life without Mel, and remembering what he had been without her, he prayed that he would never have to find out.

He was often amazed by the amount of friends Mel still had from college, although compared to Keith, simply remembering a face in a yearbook would have put her up by ten. When they shopped for their first apartment, she had known a broker that found a great deal for them. A guy that had tried to date her once now owned a car dealership, and they bought their first new car together for less than used. An idea about possibly building a house dredged another "old school chum", this time one of the top architects in the state. Designs and blueprints were had for a song. An actual song mind you, for all that Keith and Mel had to do was to go to a Karaoke party at this friend's lodge out in the wilderness.

Upon arriving, Keith had found a place on the earth that mirrored his soul. Quiet, open and with little trace of humanity, other than the odd neighbor every three to four miles, he excitedly told Mel that this was where he wanted them to live, for the rest of their lives. Absolutely astonished to see her husband beaming like this, she agreed to think about the possibility. Three months later, their cabin was being built. Keith decided that he wanted to oversee the construction of the home, partly due to his natural distrust of other people, and also because he really didn't want to go back to their apartment in Ann Arbor. Mel would become frazzled when Keith acted like this, but she knew that once he dug his feet in on something, there was no talking him out of it. Besides, wasn't this the side of him that attracted her in the first place? The cabin came together without incident, and living within it was exactly as Keith had imagined.

Mel was painting less, but her gallery in the city was thriving. She lived for discovering new talent, for being able to be the step up for so many. The entire den of Keith and Mel's home was filled with "thank yous" from the artists that had gotten their first break from Mel. She had cut her schedule down to visiting the gallery only three times per week, because she wanted to spend more time just being in their home, enjoying their life together.

Thursdays were Mel's third day at the gallery, and a rainy, autumn type found her in an odd mood. She didn't feel like getting out of bed, and was having a hard time getting motivated. Knowing his wife for the morning person that she was Keith wondered if she wasn't catching a bug of some kind.

"You know, I just got over that flu two nights ago, maybe I gave you some."

"I love you, honey, but germs aren't necessarily the type of sharing I expect from you. No offense." Mel replied.

"That hurts, babe. We swap spit frequently, you know." Keith teased. Mel half-grinned after that comment, and seemed to be lifting. A large glass of chocolate milk and her daily bowl of Cocoa Pebbles also helped immensely. Keith sat down at the table with his paper and a cup of tea and marveled at the beautiful woman opposite him inhaling kids' cereal.

"What?" Mel asked, realizing that she was being mentally photographed.

"You eat like a six-year old. Christ, do you know how much shit is in that stuff?" He asked, laughing.

"Yes, and that's why it has this lovely shade of brown, too. Get off my ass, Randall."

Keith roared, hoping that tea was not spraying from his nostrils. Mel began to laugh, also, and the whole morning seemed to rise a bit. "I've got to go in today, honey. This new naturalist is supposed to be bringing some samples to me, so I need to be there. I promise that I will get out as soon as I can."

"Why don't you give me a call when you're about to leave? Then, I can get either lunch or dinner ready for us." Keith asked. Mel agreed and stood up. As she straightened, Keith re-affirmed his basic belief that the sexist thing a woman can wear to bed is her husband's dress shirt. Catching the look in his eyes, Mel couldn't help but play a little. "You know what? I think I'll just throw on my jeans and a ball cap, and go in like so.

You won't miss this shirt, will you?" She teased. Keith grinned and reached across the table to grab her. He caught the tail of the shirt and pulled Mel toward him.

"I won't miss the shirt as long as what's inside comes back."

Mel giggled. "Do you realize how much I truly love you? Do you?"

"Well, I know that you saved my life that day on campus. I was traveling down a very dark path, you know. And I know that it takes an awfully large amount of selflessness and love to reach the type of bitter curmudgeon that I was becoming." Keith answered.

"Can't you just say yes?" she questioned. "Are you sure that you weren't an English major? You should try writing."

"Maybe I will, Mel. But only when you can't support us anymore."

"Asshole." Mel laughed and glanced at the clock on the stove. "I've got to get dressed, Keith, I'm running late. Be a dear and clean up breakfast?" Keith nodded, and started to clear the dishes. Walking to the sink, he noticed that his wife was as good as her word, for she had put her jeans and Keith's Titleist cap on along with the shirt that she had worn to bed. "I realized that it was a good idea," Mel said, gesturing toward her ensemble. "Besides, this shirt smells like you, and that's really nice on the trip to town... makes me feel like you're with me."

"My, but you're a romantic when you're rushing out the door. Be careful driving, and get out quickly. Don't forget to call when you leave, okay?"

"I won't. Gotta go hon." Mel said, and kissed Keith on the forehead. "Love you!"

"I love you, Mel."

The phone rang sometime around one o'clock, but the voice on the other end when Keith answered did not belong to Mel. A young man, stammering as he spoke, asked if he had reached "Mr. Keith Randall". When Keith confirmed this, the young man began to tell him that there had been an accident. The young man was a police officer, and was the first on the scene of a vehicle collision near the Oliphant Art Gallery. A delivery truck had run a red light, plowing into the side of a yellow convertible owned by a Mrs. Melanie Randall. The sound of Keith's throat catching must have been audible over the phone, because the officer paused, then asked Keith's permission to continue. The truck pushed the car another one hundred feet before both vehicles came to a stop against a brick wall. The truck driver was pronounced dead on arrival at St. Mary's. The responding ambulance team had determined Mrs. Randall's death had been nearly instantaneous. The officer assured Keith that Mel didn't suffer, and said that he was very sorry for Keith's loss.

Most of this information would be recalled at the kitchen table along with a bottle of bourbon, because Keith went on autopilot after the policeman had said the word "accident" and "Melanie".

Everything became a blur. Mel's Aunt Ginnie helped Keith with the arrangements, and the funeral was conducted in the Catholic tradition. It was attended by a few friends and Mel's family, and all were genuinely saddened for Keith. Mel's brother Bobby held Keith by the shoulders as he tried, his body racked with sobs, to speak at the showing. Everyone assured Keith that his eloquence had served his wife perfectly, and they all gained a measure of peace and closure from his words; all of them but Keith. He ran alternately hot and cold afterward, and some days were better than others, but none more than barely tolerable.

A few weeks later, Mel's lawyer made sure that the proper procedures were followed, and Keith sold the gallery to Mel's assistant. After conferring with Aunt Ginnie and Bobby, Mel's ashes were spread on the property behind the cabin. The next day, Keith Randall dropped out of the human race, not caring if he won or lost, or even if he ever saw another runner again.

"Answer the damn phone, Keith. I swear, if you've wandered drunk into your back forty again..." Lannie let her thought drift away. She had asked herself occasionally if being tough with Keith was the right approach. Fragile he wasn't, but his internal scars from losing Mel were beginning to show outwardly. Keith's demons were his muse, but Lannie exposed them to the world. "Hmph. That's enough idle time. One more try, and if you don't answer, buddy, I'm coming to get you." She said aloud.

The publisher was very happy to take Keith's latest work. They even raved about his idea to use the anonymous picture for the book jacket, figuring that if Keith Randall did the homework, then they needn't worry about any legal ramifications. Lannie hadn't even left the office before a designer was on the elevator up, ready to spout endless ideas on the best cover imaginable.

"Oh my God Lannie! I've never been called on to do one of HIS books." Squealed some flake from design on his way into the office.

"He's not *God* dear, in fact he won't even answer his freaking phone!" Lannie shouted, really to no one in particular. "Fine. I'm coming to get you, Keith, and if you're laying face down in elk shit again, I am not cleaning you up." With that statement made, again, to nobody save herself, Lannie headed to the parking garage. The little voice inside her head kept repeating a simple mantra: "Save the meal-ticket, save the meal-ticket..." but was she that shallow? That query was on her mind as she pulled her Dodge out into traffic. It was almost a three-hour drive to Keith's cabin Up North, so there would be time for introspection. Every now and then, she liked to catalog herself, see where she was at compared to where she thought she should be.

Lannie was halfway to forty, never married and with no children. She became an agent by accident, really. Bright and funny and blessed with a beautiful voice, Lannie wanted to be a star. As talented as she was; her self-esteem was horrible. She got together with Andy Reyes right after high school, mostly because she wanted to put her life in someone else's hands, but her friends warned her about moving too quickly and her family was non-supportive. Lannie's answer to their concern was to pack and move across the country with Andy, thinking that the distance would be a salve to all her worries and problems. What it became was a wake-up call, served to her in the form of a backhanded slap from Andy.

Andy drank too much, a condition that he had kept hidden from Lannie. He also hid the fact that his violent temper liked to flare out of control, manifesting itself in blows to Lannie both physical and emotional. The last secret was revealed one evening after they went to bed. Andy rolled over and looked deep into Lannie's eyes. She was going to tell him that she loved him, but he shushed her and simply said, "Baby, I don't love you, and I never will, but we can still screw, right?"

That was it. Three strikes and Lannie was out. She got out of bed, grabbed a suitcase while Andy's protests fell on deaf ears, and left. She walked to the bus station, tears streaming down her cheeks, bought a ticket, and headed back home. She arrived to a warm welcome, and found no choruses of "I told you so" waiting. Unfortunately, reality has a nasty way of hitting you like a shovel between the eyes at times like this. Alone, with no job, little money, and sadly, no dreams any longer, she saw her lot as akin to that famous baby that was stuck in the well. But there was no media attention or a selfless rescue crew for this girl, and if she were going to get past this, it would be on her own.

An escapade to the local bar reawakened her voice, when a Budweiser-fueled bravado and a dare from a friend got Lannie in front of an open mike on karaoke night. She began quietly, and self-consciously, and was met with a few claps of approval. Steeled, she asked for a jazz standard to be played next, and when the first clarinet note came slinking from the amplifier, Lannie was ready. All of the hurt, the disillusionment and self-doubt buried inside acted like a rocket booster for her voice, and suddenly, she was a lioness, and she could roar.

Karaoke night soon led to nights and then to weeks. Lannie would drive around the city, looking for any bar or club that would allow her to experience that feeling again. As she went from stage to stage, her audience grew, and so did the applause. She fed off it, and the changes to her personality were huge. Her confidence kept growing, and she gained strength that she thought she'd never have. She started telling people how to do things and giving good advice, whether at the tavern or the supermarket. Other singers would seek her out, asking for her to accompany them to auditions for emotional support. That had brought her to her current calling, when a director said that "if not for Lannie, he wouldn't have seen the client".

"Client? But, but I'm not an agent..." she stuttered at the time.

"Oh well, back to the here and now, Lannie. Only an hour left to Keith's cabin." The switch to the book world was made because she couldn't bear to watch the dreams of young people end. Not that she had a perfect record with publishers, either, but you could be an effective literary agent at much longer distances, and not have to be touched by the plights of the unknown. Keith was different, though. Perhaps divine intervention caused her to be the person that answered when he had called her office. "You're the first ad in the magazine," Keith would tell her later, "that's why I picked you."

He had demanded that she be the only one he would talk to, and said that he would *not* come to her office, and *she* would have to come to his home. He would give her the manuscript if she was interested, and all following transactions could be conducted through phone, mail and fax.

Lannie was intrigued, and accepted the conditions. She drove to the boondocks, got the manuscript, and was summarily blown away by it. She signed Keith immediately, and was rewarded with the first best seller in her stable. Keith's second novel arrived the same way, and resulted in similar sales. Book number three was unique in the fact that Lannie had persuaded Keith to send her a picture that she could use for the jacket, albeit one from his first-grade class composite photo. She finally peeked inside Keith's home when she needed an immediate re-write on two chapters for his fourth novel.

Even then, by the time that Lannie had arrived at his cabin, Keith simply met her at the door with the pages in his hand, smiling like a canary-fed tomcat. "You're very cute for a nutcase, you know that, Keith?" Lannie remembered saying. Keith's face got cloudy then, and he brusquely waved her away.

Following the printing of that book, Lannie finagled herself another visit to 'Casa Randall', and actually got Keith to talk about himself. He made her agree that no one else would hear what he would say, and then told her only about Mel. Noting the way that Keith seemed to retreat even further inward as he spoke, Lannie realized that she was seeing first-hand the very thing that allowed Keith to write the dark things that he did so effectively. It stunned her to see no physical change in Keith as he told the story, but she didn't know that three people died the day that Mel's car was crushed, one just hadn't been laid to rest.

Everything looked the way it always did as Lannie made the turn into Keith's drive. The cabin was still gorgeous, as was the view of the surrounding land. Keith's truck sat near the garage, and a lazy snaggle-toothed tabby was sleeping on the hood. She parked next to the Chevy, eliciting only a bored yawn from the cat.

"Hello, Mack." she said, stopping to scratch the cat's ears. At the mention of his name, Mack jumped down and started toward the front door of the cabin, pausing every few feet to turn in Lannie's direction and meow.

"I'm coming, I'm coming. Jeez, you're as bad as your master, aren't you?" The door was unlocked, as usual, and Lannie walked in, announcing herself. "You won't answer your phone, so I made an executive decision and came to get your sorry butt." No answer was returned. Looking around, she was heartened to see that nothing had changed in the make-up of Keith's home. The walls that had once held Mel's artwork were bare, and the rest of the home was spartan indeed. The cabin was clean, but completely unwelcoming; similar to a museum diorama and in its own way it was just as intriguing. She heard faint music coming from the direction of the kitchen and headed that way. She saw Keith slumped in the chair as soon as she crossed the threshold and was instantly nauseous. "Oh God, Keith. Not now…"

Three

*L*annie had seen Keith in various stages of drunkenness before, so there was not much that would have surprised her, although this she would definitely be committing to memory. Somehow, Keith had managed to get his legs intertwined with the back of the chair, and was lying face up on the floor. Today his accomplices were the empty bottles of Labatt's Blue standing defiantly on the table and an empty stomach, judging by the lack of dishes or pots and pans in the sink. "God, Keith, it's only two o' clock." Lannie mumbled. She started toward him, intending to raise him from his stupor, but Mack beat her to it. Meowing loudly, the cat pounced on Keith's head, shocking him awake and nearly causing him to split the chair in half with his flailing legs.

Lannie laughed aloud while Mack, proud of the job he'd done, pranced off toward the hall, still meowing. "Hmm... maybe I need to put that cat of yours on retainer, Keith. He got you moving quicker than I ever have. Perhaps you forgot to feed him or something?" Lannie said, still laughing.

"Shut up, Lannie. Damn cat!" Keith yelled at the hallway. He brought himself to his feet, and stumbled toward the sink. He was wearing a sweatshirt and jeans, but no socks and his hair appeared to be hosting a nest-building convention. Lannie surmised by his condition that Keith had spent last night without the company of sleep.

"Was the blue crew on the table from last night, or was that breakfast?"

Fortunately, Keith had his head under the faucet, and his reply sounded mostly like "gub fub yubsub".

Toweling his hair, he began a less cryptic response. "Why are you here, Lannie? I didn't call you and I know that you didn't call me. So what use do I have for you?" He pulled the now-damp sweatshirt over his head and slung the towel around his shoulders.

Chopping wood and working on his property had forced Keith into excellent shape, and Lannie had a hard time pulling her eyes from his torso. He was still handsome, but in an "I couldn't give a shit" way. He cut his own hair in a cropped style and was clean shaven, but Lannie knew that his hard features must have been softer when Mel was still around.

"I won't take that last part personally, because usually you have no use for anybody. Anyway, I did call, you didn't answer, and I got worried. I assumed that you'd gotten drunk again and wandered out into the wilderness. Not that your past behavior would have led me to that conclusion." Lannie rolled her eyes for effect on the last comment, hoping to get a rise out of Keith. Her effort failed. He walked to the stereo system and stopped the *Refreshments* disc mid-song, but only after his favorite line faded. "I'm just waiting for this coal-black soul of mine… to come alive…" he mumbled.

"If only that were true." Lannie thought aloud. Keith shot her a fierce look but she ignored it. "Look Keith, all I want to do is be a good agent; I don't want to tell you how to live. I figured that you would want to know that the publisher loves the book, and they're green-lighting the entire project. 'Kaycee Landing' will be the hottest romance writer around within two weeks. I'm handling all the press; so don't worry about anyone finding out who really wrote the book. Now, having said what I wanted to say, I will get out of here."

Lannie shook her head as she walked to the door. She wanted to stay, to talk to Keith and maybe even get him to listen. Something had gotten him to write that romance, something that he probably hadn't touched upon since Mel died. Whether he knew it or not, the words that flowed from him in his newest book were beautiful.

It was full of life and hope, and so spiritually re-affirming that Lannie read the manuscript three times before she truly believed that it came from Keith. She turned and looked at Keith, wondering how a human being so driven to self-destruction could tap into a vein of pure bliss, even if it was only for the duration of a novel. "Who did you used to be, Keith?" she asked. "The little bit that you've told me about Mel leads me to believe that you loved her so much that it hurt. Don't you think you're poisoning those memories now? Don't you…"

"Shut up, Lannie!" Keith yelled, cutting off her thought. "Just shut up! I don't wake up in the morning without tears in my eyes. The day that Mel was killed, *we* died, this *life* died." He raised his arms as if to envelope the entire cabin. "*I* died." He was shaking, and not just from the booze. Exhausted, Keith lifted his head and Lannie could see the tears streaming past his cheeks. "The new book? I know you're curious about it. I felt her. I felt Mel, her presence, her soul, stronger than I have in years. I could feel her arms around my chest, and I could hear her voice in the room." He sobbed. Lannie felt water on her chin and realized that she was now crying. She wanted to do something, but she was unsure of the "correct" procedure. Keith began to seethe again as he sniffled and continued talking. "I never dedicated any of my other books to her, you know. I didn't want that *darkness* associated with her. But that story was hers; those words were bursting with her, full of her light, and it felt so good to channel them. When I finished, I felt such calm and peace. I even made a joke when you picked it up, Lannie. Then it stopped. As soon as you took those final pages with you, Mel was gone... again!" He bellowed the last statement and knocked the table over, sending beer bottles and papers flying. He whirled on his heels and fell in a heap to the floor, his hands on his head. In a tear-stained voice he croaked, "Don't you see, I let her die again. I let her die again."

Lannie quietly closed the door of the den, where Keith had been sleeping since Mel died, and padded lightly down the hall. She had helped him to bed and drawn the shades, hoping that even a few minutes of unconsciousness would allow him to function again. She had seen drunks before; from Andy to the nameless members of the barstool union, but none had ever spiked the way that Keith did. The rage and the guilt that poured from him were staggering. Lannie had seen him fighting both of those emotions in the kitchen, and the scene very nearly broke her heart.

"Ugh. Why do you drink this stuff, buddy?" she wondered aloud as she cleaned the broken glass from the tile. She could imagine the warmth that the cabin had when it was still a home; when Mel was still alive. Now, in its sterile state it was just somewhere to exist, and Lannie shivered with the chilled that she imagined were emanating from the walls.

She righted the table and sat down and half-smiled when Mack rubbed against her leg. He meowed quizzically at her and was rewarded with a perch on her lap. While she scratched the tabby's ears, her mind raced, hurdling from question to question. Why did Keith feel Mel all of a sudden? Why was he trying to drink himself to death? Why did he shoulder the blame for her dying? It was all so maddening. One of the things that Lannie prided herself on was her ability to actually care about her clients, to be a friend and help when necessary, but Keith refused to let her.

After the first conversation that Keith and Lannie had, she did a little legwork. On her way back to her office, she stopped at the gallery that Mel had owned. Fortunately, Mel's old assistant still ran the place. Lannie had introduced herself and had gotten on quite well with the owner. When the subject turned to Mel, the man could not have been more glowing in her reminiscing. But the Keith that he described was not the Keith that Lannie knew. The owner and Keith had met only a few times, but the owner painted him as romantic yet mysterious. A man with stars in his eyes and a smile as broad as the moon when he watched his wife, yet who was full of ice and steel when confronted by strangers. "He didn't care for people, but his wife, oh that was a mythical kind of love." Lannie had remembered the man saying.

Mack's tooth scraping her finger brought Lannie back to the here and now. She shook her head and looked the cat in the eye. "How did your master get to this place, Mack? Better yet, where is he going next?"

"Meow?"

Stretching, and then realizing that she could do no more, other than fill Mack's bowls, Lannie grabbed her keys and coat and headed for the door. She'd poured the rest of Keith's beer down the drain, and Mack had pointed out the two bottles of schnapps hidden behind the water heater, both of which were also part of the area water table now. She knelt and kissed Mack on the head, then locked the door behind her and stepped into her truck. When she got back to the office, she would call the publisher and lie that Keith was all for the big treatment that the book was going to get, and couldn't be happier that the press wouldn't be looking for him at all with this one.

Pulling on to the highway, Lannie looked beside her at the mock-up for the book jacket that she had brought with her. She was glad that she didn't take it into the cabin when she saw Keith, knowing that in the state he was in, he probably would have shredded it. Lannie stared at the photo and into the eyes of the beautiful woman whom Keith had named Kaycee Landing, asking questions that couldn't be answered. "Did Mel come to Keith through you, my dear?"

When Keith's publisher wanted to get things done, they were done quickly, and the new book project was on top of the "get done" list. Within a week, an initial shipment of the book had been printed and a regional release dated secured. Twelve cities in the east would receive the books first; hopefully creating a huge buzz that would have readers craving the first romance from Kaycee Landing. The chain stores had gotten advance point of purchase displays and floor cutouts heralding the arrival. Amazon already had the book at number three on its list, based on pre-orders only. "A Love Worth Living" was going to make gobs of money for the publisher, but it would throw a gorilla-sized monkey wrench into the gears of Keith's life.

Four

"Oh my God, that girl on the poster looks just like you, Kris. I mean exactly! Come look at this!"

"Donna, the bookstore's closed, how am I going to look at anything?" Kris answered. She had agreed to start walking with Donna in order to support her desire to get in shape, but it seemed that Kris got the workout, whereas Donna got to window shop through the mall without having to fight the crowds. "Okay, how much could this person really look like…me…" her voice trailed off as she saw the display. This can't be right, she thought as she stared at the poster. Suddenly, she felt the sensation of being sucked into a time warp. The reason that the woman in the poster resembled Kris was because she was Kris. "Donna, that *is* me. That's from when I was in college, when I was trying to model. I did a shoot that was going to be sold to a picture frame company, and that's the picture! Oh my God!"

"Unbelievable," laughed Donna. "Kris Helton, meet Kaycee Landing. I'm sure that the two of you have a lot to talk about." A lot was an understatement, and Kris was starting to move on from astonishment into full-blown indignation. She kept wondering how this all was possible, how her face could be on the jacket of a book that she knew nothing about. Then Kris smacked her forehead, remembering signing away the rights to the photos. While waiting for the store to open, her eyes periodically fixed on those of her two-dimensional counterpart and Kris tried to imagine what she would find inside the novel. Lost in thought, she didn't see the shocked look on the face of the employee behind the glass. Soon, there was another, then another, until six workers were pressing against the storefront, asking each other why no one told them that the author was going to be in town. Kris' attention became re-focused when she heard the gate being unlocked. A young woman with a quavering voice and a shy smile asked Kris politely to come inside. "None of us realized that you were going to be here for the release of your book, Ms. Landing, and as store manager, I heartily apologize for not being prepared. Now, is there anything that we can get for you?"

"Well, Miss…"

"Anne, Ms. Landing. Anne Gables."

"Well, Anne, I suppose the first thing that you could do is help me figure out how my picture is on a book that I didn't write." Kris answered. She would snicker later at the way the pale young woman became almost transparent after Kris made her statement. "My name is Kris Helton, not Kaycee Landing, but that is me in the picture on that book jacket," Kris looked around, "Not to mention the poster in the window, the cards on the table, and the bookmarks at the register. Now Anne, I don't expect you to know how this all came about, and if you don't mind, I would like to purchase one of these books so I can continue my own investigating." The manager handed a book to Kris and told her that it was on the house. Kris thanked her and walked through the gate, grinning as she heard it close and lock behind her. Even though Kris was furious about the situation that she found herself in, holding a book in her hand that carried her face was an amazing feeling. She was suddenly very glad that she had taken two weeks of vacation from the insurance company; she had a strong craving to devour this book and glean any information from its pages. Donna had waited patiently for Kris to complete her business in the bookstore, and wanted to see the object of Kris' irritation.

"Wow. '<u>A Love Worth Living</u>', huh? Sounds like a romance. Now I know that you didn't write this." Donna teased. "Although, I think that you look better now than you do in that picture. How old were you?"

"When the picture was taken? Twenty-one." Kris answered. "My junior year of college, and I needed money badly. That's why I signed off my rights to the photo. They said they would pay me two grand right then, so I took the deal. Thanks for the compliment, though." The evidence bore out Donna's flattery however. At twenty-one, Kris still looked like a high school kid, but at twenty-five, she was very much a striking woman. She stood at nearly five and a half feet, and her long hair was a beautiful shade of auburn. Her olive skin was flawless, and complimented her large, slightly almond-shaped brown eyes. She had the body of a runner, and in fact, she had competed in intramural track while she was in college. Her mind was racing faster than her body had ever run right now, though, and she needed to get her bearings before she could go on with this morning. "Let's go, Donna. You've got to get to work anyway."

"Don't rub it in. Just make sure to fill me in on anything that you find out, especially if you're going to sue or whatever."

Kris laughed. "I wouldn't have a leg to stand on, toots. Besides, right now, I just want to know who's responsible for this so I know who to get nasty at." They both chuckled, but Kris' laughter was slightly edgier. She knew that Donna didn't take this as seriously as she did, but it also wasn't Donna's picture on the book. Therefore, it wasn't Donna's life that had been invaded. The paranoid part of Kris' brain was moving in overdrive, and she was imagining the worst results possible during the ride to her home. Within ten minutes, Donna had dropped Kris at her house and had left for work. Kris made her promise not to tell anyone at the office, although she was afraid that soon it wouldn't matter if Donna said anything or not. She bounded through the front door and headed straight for the answering machine, confirming that it was still active. An even quicker shower followed a quick trip to the kitchen to brew a pot of coffee. Now extremely comfortable in her robe and slippers, Kris sat down on the sofa and mulled her next move. "Hmm. Call the publisher and raise holy hell, or read the book and decide if I want people to think I wrote it? What options." In her relaxed state, reading first won out.

Kris took a long sip from her cup and cracked open the book. She noticed the dedication first; "To Mel, this one you'll like." and wondered about the identity of "Mel". A lover or husband perhaps? Maybe a father or brother? The intoxicating mystery of the situation had softened the riled mood that she had displayed earlier, and she found herself wanting to enjoy the novel.

The story began with an old woman relating a tale of courtship between her and her equally aged husband to a couple of inquisitive grandchildren. It was a story of true love and redemption, of devotion and friendship, and one that continued unhindered into the couple's golden years. When the woman would relate how the love of her husband had saved her life, Kris cried. She even put the book down for a few moments just to reflect. She identified with the heroine on certain fronts. She also was an only child, but Kris had been spared the tragic loneliness that marked the character's early years. She was alone now, however. She still had her family and some close friends, like Donna, but Kris didn't have that one true love, either to give or receive.

She picked the book back up and didn't stop reading again until it was finished. The clock on the wall struck five, and Kris stood and stretched. The time spent was worthwhile, though, for the book was wonderful. She felt completely renewed spiritually, as if some of the love coursing through the story had found its way into

48

her soul. She still planned to call the publisher in the morning, but the other details had been altered. Kris no longer wanted to spew threats and curses at the company, but she did want to contact the real author. She needed to know two things: one, why was Kris' photo the one chosen, and two, whose love story was this?

Morning came altogether too quickly for Kris, and the previous day's cramming of information resulted in a throbbing headache. She rolled out of bed, tangling her leg in the blanket and ending the entire maneuver on her rear end with a resounding thud. "Ouch! Damn blanket! What time is it, anyway?" she groggily asked herself. She lifted her head from the floor and stared at the clock, waiting for her eyes to focus on the glowing green numbers. The clock stared back at Kris with a bright reading of 5:44. "Oh, why am I awake? I'm on vacation, for goodness sake." Then, as solidly as her bottom had struck the floor, memory hit her square in the face. It was the book. Remembering this filled Kris with a renewed sense of purpose and energy that belied the early hour.

She jumped to her feet, shed the robe and slippers that she had worn to bed and ran to her bathroom. While the water warmed, she turned up the CD player mounted under her medicine cabinet as loud as she could and stepped into the shower. The water was hot, very hot, and exactly as Kris preferred it. She felt that a steaming hot shower always helped clear the fog from her brain and she definitely wanted to be lucid today.

Bouncing under the spray as the music pounded, Kris began to daydream about what she might find out on her trek. She imagined that she would receive the information that she needed from the publisher without a hitch, and that she used that knowledge to track down the kindest, gentlest woman the world had ever known. She dreamed that the woman would apologize to her for the use of the photograph, and that she had used it only on the advice of her agent. Then, the woman would welcome Kris into her home, and reveal that the love story in the novel was indeed hers, and she and Kris would talk for days, becoming the closest of friends. The more Kris thought about it, the more excited she became. She was almost giddy as she stepped to the mirror to brush her long hair. She paused long enough to look her reflection in the eyes, and say, "This is it, kid. You are going to find yourself, in more ways than one." The reflection laughed, and Kris was happy. Happier than she had been in months. She pulled on a Henley and a pair of jeans, and then grabbed the phone in order to call Donna. The message that Kris left on Donna's voice mail rambled a bit, but the gist of the situation was there. She was going wherever she needed to go to find out whatever she needed to find out. Four outfits similar to what she was currently wearing then flew into a large duffle, along with some new underwear, a pair of cut-offs, assorted toiletries and a fall jacket. "Can't plan for too many eventualities." She said to herself. Kris took two deep breaths and exhaled mightily. She threw her purse over her shoulder, clutched the duffle in one hand and her keys in the other, and walked through the house until she was on the front step. She pulled the door shut behind her, and making sure that she heard the lock click, she got into her car and drove away, not once

looking back at her home.

Five

*M*orning had also reached out and touched Lannie Reyes, albeit with all the gentleness of a brick covered in cashmere. "Why is it that every time I find Keith in a drunken stupor, I'm the one that wakes up with the hangover?" she thought as she watched the lighted numbers in the elevator go on and off with each passing floor. The publisher requested her presence at a marketing meeting that dealt with the expanding plans for the Kaycee Landing book, and refusal was not an option. She picked her briefcase from the floor of the car and readied herself for the opening of the doors as the number thirty lit. "What minor pitfalls await me today, I wonder." Lannie said under her breath while leaving the elevator. She waved at the receptionist seated by the front door, and vaguely noticed a pained look on his young, inexperienced face. Against her better nature, she turned on her heel and walked toward the desk. "What's up Timothy? You look like you did the time that you swore that Stephen King was in the lobby." Timothy gulped, and pointed toward the waiting sofa. Lannie turned to follow his fingers, and was thunderstruck by what she saw. "That woman wants to know why her picture is on our latest book Ms. Reyes, and she said she wasn't leaving until she got answers." Timothy said. Lannie rubbed her eyes and looked at the woman on the couch again. It was the woman that Keith had created; it was Kaycee Landing in the flesh, and she looked twice as good in person as she did in that damn picture. Lannie gathered her wits and shuffled over to the waiting area, trying to formulate the correct plan in her head before something stupid fell out of her mouth. "Hi. I'm Lannie Reyes, and I understand that you are looking for some information, Miss..." she started.

"Helton. My name is Kris Helton. And before I begin, maybe you should tell your secretary there that I'm not going to kill anyone. He's been very nervous since I walked through the door." Kris answered. She smiled in Timothy's direction, but the only result was the dropping of another shade of color from the young man's face.

"Please excuse Timothy, he's prone to celebrity sightings and I think that your showing up here unannounced may have sent the poor lad around the bend." Lannie said cordially. She kept smiling at Kris, trying desperately to kick-start her brain into action, wanting it to create a feasible plan. A plan, hopefully, that would make everyone happy. "You know Miss Helton, you bear an uncanny resemblance to our newest author, Kaycee Landing. Are you related, perhaps?" Lannie asked, figuring that the head-on approach was her best bet. The look on Kris' face however, suggested otherwise.

"Related? That's cute. Technically, you could say that I am, because that's me in that picture, not Kaycee Landing. Coincidentally, that photo is why I'm here. I want to know who Kaycee Landing is, and why she's using my face to sell her book." As Kris finished her statement, she felt stronger, surer of herself. She was determined to get to the bottom of this mystery, and even though her cause was not vindictive, Kris was ready to play the "nasty card" if it was necessary.

Lannie was taken aback by this last exchange, and she realized that the possibility of Kris being right was very high. Either Kris Helton was the young woman in the photo, or she was an excellent con who had done a lot of homework. Lannie was about to question Kris to find out what exactly she knew when her cell rang. "Excuse me for just a few seconds, Miss Helton, while I take care of this. Hello?" Lannie answered, hoping beyond hope that the voice on the other end would belong to Keith. When she heard blues music in the background, she breathed a heavy sigh of relief.

"Okay, I know that I was drunk, and I know that you were here. Now, why was I fully clothed in bed?" Keith asked, still a bit groggy from his last binge. "Did I throw you out and stumble there myself, or did you drag me there? And how did you find my schnapps?"

"My, but you're inquisitive when you're hung over. I *helped* you to your bedroom, so that's one, and two; Mack told me about the booze. While you are trying to process that information, here's another mind-blowing fact. Kaycee Landing is standing ten feet in front of me, right this moment. The real Kaycee Landing." Lannie listened, wondering how Keith would react. The sound of him spraying out whatever he had been drinking was very satisfying, but she allowed herself only the smallest of smiles, for this situation was becoming very serious, very quickly. "Are you there, Keith?" She asked. Keith was thunderstruck. He could not imagine how the woman in the photo that he had so arbitrarily picked could actually be at the publisher's building. He almost had a desire to drive into the city and see her in person, but that passed almost quicker than it emerged.

"When I called to check on the legality of using that picture Lannie, I was assured that everything was on the up and up. That nobody could contest its use or try to sue me. What does she want? Does she still look like the picture? What..." Keith started before Lannie interjected.

"Hold it, sport. Only one answer at a time. The legal department checked the usage and it is okay. Next, all that she has asked for is information, why the author used her picture, precisely. Lastly, she looks better in person, if for some reason that's important to you." Lannie finished with a slight huff. She wanted to grill Keith more about the anxiety that he was displaying over the phone, but it would be easier to do that in person. Besides, she needed to deal with Kris first. "I will call you back, Keith, as soon as I get things under some semblance of control. Bye."

"If you need a few moments, Ms. Reyes, I can continue to make your receptionist sweat." Kris said with an impish grin. The fact that she was enjoying this was evident, both in the size of her smile and the sparkle in her eye. From the instant that she stepped from the elevator and sent Timothy into a palsied state, Kris had felt confident and in control. She measured Lannie with her gaze, knowing that she was already trying to hide something. Kris waited for Lannie to send Timothy to the lounge for a break, and then began again. "Okay, Ms. Reyes, why is Kaycee Landing using my picture to sell her book? Is she old? Is she spectacularly homely? Why me? And I believe that someone here owes me an answer." She set her jaw and steeled herself for the evasive action that she expected to get from Lannie.

"Well, Miss Helton," Lannie began, "First of all, I have no proof that Kaycee Landing is not the woman on the book jacket. Yes, you are a very lovely young woman and you do bear a striking similarity to Kaycee. However, I would guess that ten percent of the female population might look like Kaycee, and if you are looking to make a financial windfall by looking like someone, I can assure you that that is just not going to happen." The tough approach was normally what Lannie adopted in situations of this type, and she was hoping that she could squash Kris quickly and cleanly.

Kris simply nodded and smiled at Lannie, then spoke.
"I don't want any money, Ms. Reyes. I signed away my
rights to future considerations on that photo, and
therefore I know that I don't have a legal leg to stand
upon. What I want is hopefully a much simpler request
for you to grant. I want to find the woman that wrote
this book. I want to talk to her and get to know her.
Have you read this novel yet? It is amazing. The voice
speaks so clearly, and the love written about inside is
nearly overwhelming. That's what I want. The person
responsible for this beautiful story." Lannie gasped.
The book was everything that Kris described, and
Lannie wanted to agree with each statement that was
made. But meeting Keith was unacceptable. He
wouldn't allow it, and if Lannie's suspicions were
correct and Keith had chosen Kris' picture due to a
loneliness for Mel, she wouldn't allow it either. "I have
read the book, Ms. Helton, and it is wonderful, but the
author is a recluse, and trust me, someone that you
truly don't care to know. That is all I have to say on this
matter, and you will get no more information from the
publisher or me. If we have no further business, I have

an important meeting to get to, and I suggest that you leave." Lannie said flatly. She swept up her briefcase and walked past Kris, into the elevator. As quickly as the doors closed, she was dialing Keith's number. Kris frowned. She had thought that she was getting somewhere, but didn't expect to run into a toughie like Lannie. She paced around the room, trying to decide on her next move. Kris was certain that Lannie had already alerted anyone in the know at the office about her, and most of the next moves that she could make were going to lead her directly into roadblocks. Out of the corner of her eye, Kris noticed movement. She turned and saw Timothy sit down at his desk, returning from his imposed break. He smiled weakly in Kris' direction, but didn't look any less worse for wear. A devilish look crossed Kris' face as she determined her strategy. "Timothy," she started, "Do you know where Ms. Reyes was going in such a rush?" The young receptionist slowly gulped and answered. "I don't think I can tell you that, ma'am."

"Well, that's all right. I'll just go down to the street and follow her car. I just know she drives that Jaguar that I saw."

"No, she has a red Dodge Durango and... and I just screwed up, didn't I?" Timothy asked, sheepishly. Kris smiled warmly and replied,

"Yeah, but don't worry. I won't tell." She leaned over the desk and kissed Timothy lightly on the forehead, then ran out of the office and into the elevator. "I'm not giving up that easily, Ms. Reyes. You have something that you don't want me to find out about Kaycee Landing, and I going to know just what that something is." Kris thought aloud. She punched the button marked "basement", hoping that the building included an underground parking facility. The lift jerked, then began its descent. While she dropped, Kris checked her wristwatch, trying to gauge how much time had passed between the moments that Lannie left the office and her own exit. "Come on, come on..." she said, watching the lighted numbers steadily decrease. A disheartening vision in her head of an elderly doughnut-eating janitor was quickly dashed as the elevator doors opened revealing rows of shining sedans. Kris stepped into the garage just in time to watch the taillights of a truck turn the corner. "Arrgh!" she shouted, and ran the opposite direction, hoping to beat the vehicle to the street above. When she reached the street, she was rewarded with the sight of two red sport utility vehicles driving away from her; one was turning left and the other turning right. Kris glowered at the trucks, and then threw her purse to the sidewalk. "Now what?"

Lannie was sure that Kris would try to follow her, and the fervor with which she was driving resembled the leisurely pace of a robbery getaway. Her main line of thinking was to get to Keith's cabin before anyone else and attempt to formulate a con job to get rid of Kris Helton. Lannie hoped that Keith hadn't started drinking yet, for she was going to need him to be clear-headed. This wasn't the same thing as leading the tabloids on a wild goose chase with planted clues, this was personal. The woman had her own reason to search for Keith, even if she didn't realize who she was exactly looking for, and people with personal investment rarely give up easily. She couldn't think, and the events of a few moments replayed in her mind. Lannie was genuinely shocked to see Kris in the waiting room; "Kaycee Landing" in the flesh, so to speak. She was even more shocked when Kris was so engagingly cordial and nice. Nicer than she needed to be, Lannie thought. She tried to read an agenda in Kris' eyes, something that would expose her as a money-hungry witch or a person with litigation on her mind, but she could not dig deep enough. All that Lannie saw was a lovely young woman who was earnestly seeking answers. "I wonder what she'd think of Keith?" she thought aloud, still trying to decide what to tell Keith when she arrived at the cabin. "Well, if this is the biggest of our problems, we should survive."

Meanwhile, after kicking an innocent trashcan for her missing Lannie's truck, Kris jogged to the nearest pay phone and called Donna. Her plan was simple: convince her best friend to look up the auto policy on Lannie Reyes, thereby getting Lannie's license number and address. She would then call upon Lannie at home, and make her case for meeting Kaycee Landing. After promising Donna a full disclosure on all events hereafter, plus agreeing to try to get Sandra Bullock to play Donna in the movie that was surely going to made from this escapade, Kris got the information. As she hung the phone back on the clip, a sudden pang of conscience stopped her. She had felt used and invaded the first time that she saw her face on the book's jacket, and now she was about to invade someone else's life in order to gain control of hers. It was an interesting argument that Kris was having with her moral center, but the tantalizing fantasy of a new and better life lay in finding Kaycee Landing, and in the end, that fantasy won. Following a brisk run back to her car, Kris was ready to play detective. "Okay, Ms. Reyes, if you want to play hardball, we'll play hardball. But you have to go home sooner or later, and when you do, I'll be waiting."

The drive from Ann Arbor to Casa Randall is long, and not particularly exciting. There are a few towns between the two points, and a lot of blacktop. The township that surrounds Keith's home amounts to about ten thousand acres of unforested land. There is a convenience store with gas and groceries, a tiny post office, a bar, the "Fall Right Inn" and a few people that deal with Keith. A store worker delivers his groceries, and the mailbox at the end of his driveway receives his mail. The only person that Keith had to deal with on even a semi-regular level was Lannie, and she was sometimes too frequent. Little did Keith know that the carefully traced route of his life since his wife's death was soon to hit a hairpin curve.

Six

oone Arloe, or "Boo" to his friends, was sitting at
his favorite table at the coffeehouse. He enjoyed
the table in the back where he could sit for hours and
watch everybody else walk through the door,
imagining the thoughts in their heads. It also was a
prime reading spot, the owner had a deal with a big
book company which allowed him to stock brand-new
books as quickly as the chain stores could, and since
Boo was one of his best customers, the owner let him
have first pick.

"Latest releases, Boo." The owner said, dropping a loaded cardboard box onto the table. Boo smiled at him and sifted through the contents. Most of the books were the non-fiction, self-help type. A short story collection caught Boo's eye and he grabbed it, not quite noticing the book beneath. The owner shook the box, signaling that there was one item remaining. Upon peering into the box, Boo knew exactly what was left: a romance novel. The title contained the word "love", and a blue sky and white, fluffy clouds surrounded the rest of the words. He was about to dismiss the book as not worth his time, but then noticed the author's name. Boo asked the café owner if he was familiar with the name Kaycee Landing, and he told him about the big marketing push following this novel. "I've never seen a push like this for a first-timer, the story must be really good, or else this Landing chick is sleeping with the publisher. Either way, she's quite a babe." The owner offered.

"Thanks Dave. Okay, I'll try it. Maybe some romance will do me good." Boo said. As he lifted the book and turned it over in his hand, he had to agree with Dave's summation of Kaycee Landing. She was gorgeous, all long auburn hair and eyes that a man could fall into, and suddenly, Boo was much more excited about reading her book. After the server took his order, Boo held one book in each hand, as if he were a scale weighing the significance of them. He was known to devour up to three books in the time he spent at the coffeehouse, yet this day found him running late, and therefore only able to devote a few hours to his pastime. The rational mind was pushing for the collection, the literary equivalent of a lunch salad, quick, tasty, but ultimately not satisfying. On the other hand, when good, a romance novel could be like the best devil's food cake. Rich and sinful, and if you ate enough of it, it would settle into many parts of you for a long time. Still not being able to make up his mind, Boo looked skyward for assistance, but received it instead from his deepest recesses. His under-appreciated libido won the emotional tug of war, and Boo cracked the cover of A Love Worth Living. He noticed quickly that the author could turn a good phrase, and had excellent characterizations. He felt that he could hear Kaycee

Landing in every passage, and was therefore getting to know her, and know her quite well. Chapter after chapter passed before his eyes, and as Boo read, he knew that he was experiencing something that he never had before. He felt uplifted; buoyed almost, by the words on the pages in front of him. The story woven by Kaycee Landing had to be her own, Boo thought as he finished the final paragraph, staring at the jacket photo, knowing that he had to find her.

"Judging by the resemblance to Wonderland's native cat, I'd say that you enjoyed Ms. Landing's effort." Dave said, chuckling, as he walked toward Boo's table. "I fear if you grin any wider, you'll simply fade away." By this time, Dave had taken the chair opposite of Boo, and was expecting details.

"I think effortless is the word that comes to mind, Dave. It is by far the best romance that I've read. This book does not seem like the work of a first-time author. It is polished and clean, it flows like honey, and… and…" Boo stumbled, searching for the correct description.

"Go on, spit it out, Boo. Are you going to recommend it in your column for the magazine?"

"Dave, let me just say that the beauty of this book is surpassed only by the author's own. And as for the column, well, I've been considering taking a leave of absence. I just didn't have the push necessary to actually do it. Now I do. I need to find Kaycee Landing. I need to find out who this woman is, because I think that part of my destiny lies with her."

"Destiny? Did you just use that cliché?" Dave laughed. "That's absurd, man. You read a book; you didn't have a third date. But hey, if you want to tilt at windmills DQ, go for it." Dave shook his head and smiled at Boo. Half-cocked was Boo's normal state of mind, so this decision really didn't surprise Dave, but the seriousness that Boo displayed did. He was about to make another smart-aleck comment, but Boo stood from the table.

"Laugh all you want, Dave. But I know that I glimpsed into that woman's soul, and I'll be damned if I don't try to find her." Boo exclaimed, pounding the table for dramatic emphasis. He scowled at Dave, grabbed his backpack from the floor and turned to leave. He was irritated, both by Dave's comments but also by the truth that they revealed. Boo knew that he was prone to pursuing things without the virtue of thought, and there were more than a few times that he had gotten in over his head, but something told him that this was different. He had never felt a true direction in his young life, though not for lack of looking. While he was taking graduate classes in literature, Boo also held a job writing book reviews for the university press magazine, and even with great perks like free cafeteria food and the pretty freshman girls that asked him for "private tutoring", he was constantly waiting for divine intervention to start him on a new path. "Okay, Boone, the map is out, now let's make a trail." He gathered his items and confidently strode through the back door. Boo could feel the adrenaline releasing inside, and was getting more excited by the minute. He flipped the book over and looked at the photo again, and then noticed the name of the publisher. "There's my jumping on point," he said to himself, "now to do some homework." With ideas and schemes spinning throughout his mind, Boo headed back to his apartment.

Meanwhile, as another gremlin readied itself to leap into the works, Lannie arrived at Keith's home. She had been so agitated during her drive that she hadn't a clue what to tell Keith about Kris Helton. She was still trying to think of an angle when she noticed Keith walking toward her. He wore a pained expression on his face, but Lannie could smell only soap on his skin, instead of the usual boozy aroma. He was sober and obviously concerned about this unforeseen event in his life. "Hi, Lannie. What does this woman want?" Keith asked. Lannie bent down to pick up Mack, who had just joined them. As the cat nuzzled her neck, Lannie looked at Keith and replied, "I don't know Keith. She seems like a nice kid, and against my better judgment, I think she really just wants to meet the author."

"Not acceptable. You're lucky I even let you come up here, let alone some groupie." Keith spat. He was starting to get dark again, and Lannie knew that she had to keep him engaged in the situation. "Wait Keith.

Here's the kicker. She has no idea that you wrote the book, and the world at large has no idea where you are, so I don't think that you have too much to worry about. However, she appears to be intelligent, and she's tough. I could see that at the office. Why, she almost had Timothy in tears."

"Oho, shall I applaud? A three-year old could intimidate your assistant. Just tell me that she won't be bothering me. That's all I ask." He waited for Lannie to validate his request, but the reply that he got was more like, "I'll take care of it." Lannie handed Mack back to Keith, and started to get into her truck. Before she closed the door, she glared at Keith and coldly said, "You know, Keith, someday I'm going to get tired of taking your crap. Maybe if you lose someone else in your life you'll realize just how much you've let yourself die inside!" She then slammed the door shut. "Make sure Mack doesn't get run over." She offered, and then drove away. Teary-eyed, and furious at herself, Lannie watched in the mirror as Keith and Mack went back into the cabin, but turned her head before she could see the hurt in Keith's eyes as he watched her leave. She pounded the steering wheel repeatedly, trying to release some of the rage that she felt. She hadn't meant to yell at Keith, and she certainly didn't want to hurt him, but her frustration over his attitude allowed no other recourse. Besides, Lannie cared about Keith, and she was starting to fear that he was soon going to take a turn around the bend from which there was no return.

The trip home would give her ample time to cool down, but it would be late by the time she returned home. She started to push thoughts of Keith to the back of her head, and began to fantasize about a huge bubble bath and a banana split. A small grin played on her lips, and Lannie had little else on her mind for the remainder of the drive. Slightly over four hours later, Lannie shut off her truck in her own garage. She was tired, and her only plan was to see how quickly she could strip off her clothes and run her bath. She was down to her underwear by the time she made the kitchen, and grabbed a bottle of root beer from the refrigerator on the way to the tub. She took a large swallow of the soda while she waited for the water to run as hot as she could stand. With the tub then full, she removed the rest of her clothing and slid into the steaming water. Lannie laid her head back and began to think. This had been an unusual day, and she was hoping to make heads or tails of it in some way. Feeling a headache coming, Lannie decided to switch to a more philosophical pursuit; imagining what other people were doing at the same exact moment as she. "Keith's probably drunk, and Mack is sleeping on the clothes hamper." She said, somewhat dreamily. "That part is easy. I wonder what young Ms. Helton is doing right now…"

"I hate small cars! Dammit!" Kris was trying to find a semi-comfortable position in which to sleep in her car, but was experiencing no success whatsoever. Between the gear shift in her ribs and the streetlight shining through her windshield, she envisioned a long night ahead. She had used the information that Donna got from the insurance company computer to get to Lannie's house, figuring that she could go on her own stake-out, and then follow Lannie around, hoping that the trail would eventually lead to Kaycee Landing. More than once, Kris had felt the grimy sheen of dishonesty covering her, and that very feeling allowed doubt to keep poking at her plan. She tried to rationalize the situation by telling herself constantly that she was the victim in this mess. If Kaycee Landing hadn't used Kris' picture, none of this would have begun, and therefore Kris had every right to discover the truth. The repetition of these statements didn't offer Kris any real comfort, but they did allow her to focus on the job at hand, even if she was finding it more and more distasteful. Kris tried to raise her mood. "In the morning, God willing, I'll be embarking on a grand adventure. New places and new people wait, and just maybe, a new attitude as well." She looked at her reflection, and then at the book lying on the dashboard. "Goodnight, Kaycee. Goodnight Kris."

Across the city, in a book-filled apartment above Joe & Scott's Bail Bonds, someone else was excited about the coming morning. At an ornate and antique table in a corner of the room, Boone Arloe had determined his course of action. In the morning, he would arrive at the office of the publisher of Kaycee Landing' book. He would then flash his non-imposing press pass from the college magazine and announce himself as the resident literature reviewer. He would gush about the book and then humbly ask to schedule an interview with the amazing author. Then, once face-to-face with the wonderful Kaycee Landing, he could pursue both a professional and a personal relationship. It was foolproof. The only hitch was the possibility that Ms. Landing would be extremely put off by Boo's insistence and ardor. It was a possibility that he'd had in the back of his mind, because he had to admit that his plan sounded a bit "stalker-ish". "God, I hope not. This genuinely feels like something that I *have* to do." he said aloud. Boo collected the odds and ends on the table and placed them on one of the many bookshelves covering the walls. He walked to his bathroom and flipped on the light switch. He studied his reflection, watching the way the light would reveal things as he turned his head. Boo noticed a few long hairs on his chin and contemplated shaving. His last girlfriend had talked him into growing the beard that was currently residing on his jaw line, but his mom had always told him that first impressions should be made without whiskers. In the end, mom's advice won and he'd ditch the crumb-catcher. While the water in the sink ran colder, Boo smiled, and he knew that the next morning was going to bring about the start of intriguing and enlightening changes. As the razor made its road through the deep forest of hair on Boo's cheek, he started to hum one of his favorite songs. He thought about how friends find out more about one another through the time they spend together, and he had always believed that the best way to discover a lover was to find one in a good friend. Boo put down the razor and pictured the jacket photo in his mind. "I don't know why, Kaycee," he said to the vision in his thoughts, "but I feel like I've got to find you, and everything else that's waiting for me, too." He grimaced as he splashed the after-shave onto his cheeks, and then threw himself into bed, smiling from ear to ear.

Back at the cabin, Mack the cat was looking for his master. His water bowl was empty, and the condition of his food bowl was quickly approaching the same. Mack sauntered into the bedroom, trailing howls and meows behind him, hoping to wake his master. He didn't need to work that hard, however, for Keith was already awake. In fact, he hadn't yet gone to bed. A pair of French doors opened the east wall of the room to a wraparound porch, where Keith sat, peering into the darkness of the fields beyond, trying to talk to Mel. "You knew what would happen if you went first, didn't you, Hon?" he questioned the air. "That's why you wanted me to bring you out here. So I could find you if I needed to. Well, babe, I need to. I wrote another book, Mel, but this one's different. This one's about love, our love. I even dedicated this one to you, because this was the first one worthy of having your name anywhere near it. Besides, I could feel your hands on my shoulders as I wrote. I could feel you every time that I touched the keyboard. It's good, too. My agent says that its "life changing", and that she can't believe that I had that much soul inside. Here's the funny part, Mel. I didn't want to have my name on the book. I didn't think that people would buy me suddenly having a paradigm shift and getting romantic. So I took a picture out of a frame in the attic and sent that along to the publisher with the..." Keith was interrupted as Mack jumped into his lap and began purring. He scratched the tabby's chin and continued, although in a trembling voice. "The picture made me think of you when we were in college, and since the book owed so much to your presence, I felt that it was fitting." Keith wiped a teardrop from his chin, not really noticing that he had been crying. "But when I gave the manuscript to my agent, the minute she left, I couldn't feel you anymore. You were in those pages, and when I couldn't have my hands on them anymore, it was like losing you all over again. Why did I have to feel that? Why?" The last question had been yelled loud enough that Mack jumped down and ran for the safety of the house. Keith stood quickly and threw his glass into the night. As he moved to the railing, the tears ran faster and heavier down his face. Keith leaned on the railing and wailed. "I need you to come back!"

His voice echoed from the trees, mocking him. More quietly, he continued his soliloquy. "Your husband died with you, Mel, and all that's left is the bastard that I was. God, I miss you, Mel. I love you so much." Keith put his head in his hands and sobbed, hoping that somehow, some way, Mel would find her way back.

Seven

*F*ittingly, the rainstorm that assaulted Keith's cabin during the night didn't come near the city, and as the morning sun chased the remaining dusky blues and grays from the sky, Lannie woke to a serenade of songbirds accompanied by foul-mouthed garbage men. As the refuse truck stuttered and grumbled its way out of her neighborhood, Lannie was indeed grateful. "Thank heaven for small favors." She said as she climbed from her bed. "Although I truly wish that that denim-covered Neanderthal would get a grasp on a few new phrases. His act is getting old."

She hadn't slept well, but she was not as tired as she thought that she would be. She wasn't going to the office today; she had decided that spending the day with Keith would be much more effective. Lannie knew that she could talk her way into Keith's cabin, even early in the morning, and then they could spend the day brainstorming ways to deal with Ms. Helton. She also wanted the chance to apologize for her comment about Keith's losses. His psyche wasn't necessarily an open wound, but it didn't require much picking at the scab to draw blood, and Lannie felt like she had dug in with fishhook. She walked toward her bathroom, running her hands quickly and roughly through her hair until all the cobwebs had been removed from her brain. Brushing her teeth, Lannie let her mind wander back to Keith. She wished that she had known him while Mel was alive, because she knew that there were other layers of Keith that only existed around Mel. Lannie considered herself more than just an agent to Keith, even if he refused to acknowledge their friendship, and she truly wanted to help him return to the human race. The only problem was that she didn't have the first clue on how to accomplish that task. She shrugged her shoulders in quiet resignation and bent down to spit. "Damn!" she exclaimed, noticing the white stripe of toothpaste running down the front of the Red Wings sweater that she slept in nightly. "Oh man, now I've got to get this in the laundry before that crud sets!" she cried, trying to pull the jersey over her head and run to the washing machine at the same time. Hoping that no one driving by saw her running topless through the house, she blushed slightly while rubbing stain remover on the streak. "Thank goodness the garbage guys are already gone. That would have been quite embarrassing." She said, crossing the floor and stopping at the front window. She gazed into the neighborhood as she did every morning, but something new caught her eye. Directly across the street from her home, Lannie noticed a small white car that on further inspection seemed to have someone inside, sleeping. After a perusal of the headlines on the "Today" show and a large glass of grape juice, Lannie checked on the interloper again. Sure enough, the car, complete with slumbering occupant, had not moved. A devious plan hatched in her head, and she went to find her binoculars. Zeroing in on the object of her consternation, Lannie had a sudden flash of recognition, and a gasp leaped from her mouth. "Holy shit! That's Kris Helton! How in the world... I've got to get out of here and get to Keith." Lannie quickly pulled the drapes closed and threw on some clothes. Locking the front door behind her, she entered her Dodge as stealthily as she could, wanting to get on the road without alerting Kris to her departure. "Okay, Lannie, calm down. Just back out and drive away, and lovely Ms. Helton won't even stir." She eased the bright red beast into reverse and descended the driveway. Mentally patting herself on the back for regular preventative maintenance that allowed such a quiet truck, Lannie smiled, never noticing the misplaced aluminum garbage cans directly behind her in the street. The cans that were now making an unholy racket as the Durango ran them down. "Shit!" Lannie yelled, then quickly turned her head and looked at Kris' car. Her fears were realized as she locked eyes with Kris, who was wearing a dazed and groggy expression.

Recognition came to her just as Lannie slammed her truck into drive and drove off like the proverbial bat.

"Omigod...omigod. That was Lannie. THAT WAS LANNIE!" Kris screamed internally, fumbling to get the key into the ignition. By the time the car started, Lannie was already out of sight, and Kris was losing hope quickly. She spun the car around trailing smoke from the tires and sped down the street in the same direction as Lannie, hoping to catch a glimpse of her red truck. Luckily, Kris had only one choice when she reached the stop sign, and that was to turn right. Grinding gears through the turn, Kris prayed that she hadn't squandered another chance to find her imagined destiny, and as she straightened the car's path, she was rewarded with the sight of a small, bright red blur miles ahead of her. "Yes!" she yelped, "That's got to be her." Kris beamed with excitement, and her skin began to gather goose bumps as she thought about the possibility of her plan actually coming together. She closed the distance slightly, and remained there behind Lannie for twenty-five minutes, succeeding in replicating each turn that Lannie made. With the road signs signaling the interstate heading north, Kris momentarily thought that Lannie was leading her on a wild-goose chase, but quickly decided that negativity would get her nowhere, and shook the offending idea from her mind. An hour into the trip, Kris was glad that she had found a package of Pop-Tarts in the glove box; two hours into the trip and she wasn't quite sure if she was still in Michigan anymore. She knew that she hadn't crossed any state lines, but Kris had never been any further north than her childhood home in Flint, and she was starting to get nervous. The towns that she followed Lannie through got smaller and smaller, just as the distance between those towns grew. The sights were definitely prettier though, as the grays of the city gave way to the autumn reds and golds of the rural countryside. As the two vehicles joined the northbound lane of the highway, Kris' bladder could handle no more. She quickly tried to calculate the odds of losing Lannie if she were to pull over for a bathroom break, and at a welcome stoplight, Kris leveled the gaze of a speed-reader at her road map. She assumed that since the highway continued north all the way to the

Mackinaw Bridge, she could make her stop and still be able to catch Lannie. It was either that or wet herself, and meeting Kaycee Landing wearing urine-soaked pants was not what Kris had in mind. The horn of the car behind her brought Kris' mind back to the present, and she looked ahead to gauge the amount of Lannie's lead. The red truck was two stoplights in front of Kris, and not moving very quickly, due to a large livestock truck trying to turn left. She spotted a fast-food restaurant and dove into the parking lot, negotiating a small gap through the oncoming traffic. Kris left the engine running as she pulled into a spot, and bolted from the car, muttering under her breath about the perils of too much diet cola. Thankfully, the restroom was empty, and Kris received relief in record time. She was still straightening her shirt as she burst through an older couple entering the establishment, and after flinging an obligatory "sorry" in their direction; Kris sprinted to her waiting coupe eager to rejoin the chase. The dashboard clock revealed that her whole operation had cost only two minutes, and Kris was sure that Lannie hadn't been able to put many more miles between them. She eased her car back into traffic and continued the northern trek. "It's only a matter of time 'til I catch up", she thought, and a very pleased smile, not unlike that of the canary-eating feline of lore, crossed Kris' face.

"She's probably back on the road by now." Lannie mused, and checked the mileage counter on her odometer. Kris wasn't taking great pains to conceal the fact that she was following Lannie, and Lannie still hadn't decided whether to play along or to try to lose her. The determination that Kris was showing was admirable, and Heaven knew that an unexpected guest would throw Keith into a tornado-like tizzy, uprooting his carefully arranged forest of control and solitude and perhaps forcing him to confront the very demons that were dragging him into a bottomless pit. She knew she would have to choose a plan of action soon; there were only two hours remaining of the trip to the cabin, and if Lannie was going to let Kris ride her coattails, she'd need a story to feed to Keith upon arrival. "I wonder how he'll react?" Lannie wondered aloud, daydreaming slightly. Thinking about Keith always made her wistful, and she wished that she was able to reach into him more, to help him release some of the pain that he wallowed in and maybe heal a little bit of his dusty soul. "Can't reach what you can't touch, Lannie dear." She knew that Keith would likely never love again; at least not like the way it seemed that he loved Mel. It was all so maddening to Lannie, though, the entire relationship that Keith had with her. She knew how to be his agent, and she tried to be a friend, but she longed to be a confidant, someone who knew the past, and could help move the future. Lannie wasn't looking for love from Keith, at least not in the physical or marital sense, but the feelings of trust and belonging that had been missing from her own life for so long; the emotions that a person needed to truly live, rather than simply exist. Suddenly, she realized that she had made a decision through her internal dialogue. Keith was surely killing himself, either with the booze or with apathy and cynicism, and someone had to put a stop to it. An intervention was what was needed, and Lannie could think of no better way to shock Keith than by bringing a stranger into his home. It was done. Lannie would let Kris follow right up to Keith's doorstep, and hopefully bring some hope and perhaps a friendly spirit with her.

Eight

*H*appy-go-lucky people rarely discover disappointment or discouragement, and normally what little that they encounter in life is not enough to severely change their outlook. Boo Arloe was coming very close, however, to a very pessimistic view of the world. His search for Kaycee Landing had been fruitful at first, although it didn't require much deductive reasoning to find the office of the book publisher, but once there, he was finding a stone wall that he didn't anticipate meeting. "C'mon, man, can't you give me even a crumb?" he asked the receptionist.

Timothy sat ramrod straight in his chair, a steely glint in his eyes. "No. I've been instructed to say nothing about Ms. Landing, her book, or anything dealing with either of those subjects. I'm *somewhat* sorry, but if you want information, I suggest trying elsewhere. Good day, Sir." Timothy was very happy with the way that he had handled Boo, considering what happened with that Helton woman.

"Elsewhere. Great. Just great. You people sell knowledge here, and I can't get a simple question answered. Fine buddy, don't tell me anything. I'll still find her, you can bet…"

"Should I call security, sir?" Timothy asked, hoping to get a good scene to tell people about at the club later.

"Bite me. I'm leaving on my own, thank you." Boo replied, giving the receptionist the hairy eyeball. He stomped to the elevator like a bratty child being sent to bed without supper, and mentally crossed off the first idea he'd had dealing with his quest. As he punched the button for the lobby, he felt the cell phone in his pocket vibrate. The car lurched, and Boo read the message on the phone's display: "Meet me at store, I have info. Anne." Boo smiled, and felt rejuvenated. Anne Gables was living proof that parting with a girlfriend amicably was a good thing, and since she managed the bookstore in the mall, she was privy to quite a bit of industry scuttlebutt. He'd asked her to keep her ears open concerning Kaycee Landing, and hopefully that request was about to pay dividends.

When Boo got to the shopping Mecca, it was still relatively early in the morning, and although the stores didn't open their doors until ten o' clock, he could get inside through the main entrance with the everyday walkers. As he walked briskly to the bookstore's gate, Boo noticed that not all of the mall walkers were elderly, as he had first assumed. There were also a few quite attractive young women making the rounds of the center, checking their watches and the storefronts as they passed by. His name being called in a loud whisper caught his attention, and he whirled to see Anne motioning him to head her way. Boo smiled at her and galloped to the store, his momentum carrying him almost into the gate and Anne when he arrived. She gave him a friendly hug and returned his grin.

"Someone seems a bit excited..." she teased.

"I got your text and it made my morning. I hit a brick wall over at the publisher, and I was about to go stroke Dave for some of his contacts, but you came through, babe. Whatcha got?" Boo asked, breathlessly.

Anne grinned even broader this time, and replied, "Oh, I forgot what a puppy dog you are when you want something. You are so cute. And you *shaved*...! Maybe I should ask you what all this is worth, hmmm?"

"Annie! Man, I swear... Okay, as my friend and as someone who used to love me, please tell me what you've found. You have no idea how much this means to me." Boo pleaded, hoping to reach a sympathetic spot remaining for him in Anne's heart.

"I was going to tell you anyway, I just wanted to see how much you'd sweat over it." She giggled. "Anyway, this is what I know: The day that we got Kaycee Landing' book, we were all here early to put the posters and crap out, and who should come waltzing to the gate, but the author herself. She proceeds to deny the obvious fact that she was Kaycee Landing, saying some nonsense about the theft of her identity and that she wanted to buy a copy so she could 'investigate'. I gave her one on the house, and she walked out smiling. A very surreal moment in my life, may I add."

Boo's mouth hung open. "She was in your store? What kind of cosmic bad karma do I have?"

"Don't interrupt," Anne scolded. "She had a friend with her, and they were walking the mall together. I watched after she left. Now, I haven't seen Kaycee since that morning, but her friend is here every other day, usually between seven and eight-thirty. How's that for information, Mr. Arloe?" Anne waited for Boo's reaction to this good lead, hoping that he was pleased with the facts she had given him. She wasn't, however, expecting what happened next.

"Oh my God! Unbelievable! I love you Annie!" Boo yelled, and grabbed the back of Anne's head with both hands, and pulled her into a kiss that contained more passion than the entire year and a half that the two of them had dated. A dumbfounded look greeted Boo as he removed his lips from Anne's, followed by a sheepish grin. "How can I ever thank you?"

Still swaying, Anne replied, "You could stop by every once in a while and kiss me like that again, sport. Whoa. I feel like I should be asking you how you like your eggs."

"Hey, this woman, the friend of Kaycee, is she here today, have you seen her?" Boo asked, hopefully. The excitement and adrenaline were almost gushing from him, and he was having a hard time even standing still. He knew that this was the break that he was looking for, the moment that allowed him to trust that he was doing the right thing in finding Kaycee. Call it fate, coincidence or divine intervention, no matter what it was; Boo believed that he had indeed found the defining instance of his life. He looked directly into Anne's eyes, hoping to simply intuit the answer that he was looking for.

"Yes, but she's at the food court by now. Can't miss her, about five-four, bottle-blond hair and pink Hot Topic yoga pants. Good luck, Boone, I really hope this is what you want it to be." Anne reached up and hugged Boo, kissed his cheek, and then gave him a literal push in the right direction.

Donna D'Andrione set her large double espresso on the first clean table she could find. She rifled through her purse, looking for her cell phone, expecting a progress update from Kris. She choked down a large gulp of Viennese Mocha Black Walnut when the phone rang at the same moment her hand had found it, and she was still coughing as she answered the call. The voice on the other side definitely belonged to Kris, although Donna did get the impression that Kris was speaking from inside a large panel truck traveling on a dirt road. When she asked Kris about her location, a vague reply about somewhere up north was what she got. Kris was upbeat, though, because she still had a bead on Lannie's truck, and she was sure that they had to be running out of road soon. Donna laughed and mentioned to Kris that perhaps she was going to end up in the Upper Peninsula, and be stuck eating pasties for the rest of her life, married in a double-barreled ceremony to the guy in town with the most teeth. Kris didn't appreciate the joke, but continued relaying information. The last road sign that she had seen was one for "Tawas City", and she was hoping that they would find a destination quickly, because she was certain that her butt was not only asleep, but also comatose. "Hang tough, buddy…" Donna said to her friend, and requested frequent updates before she disconnected. She sat back in her chair and grinned, visualizing Kris driving along in the wilderness. She was excited for her, but a part of Donna also hoped that Kris wasn't getting into something that she couldn't handle. She exhaled the vicarious excitement and reached for her coffee. As the steam dissipated, the handsome features of Boone Arloe came into Donna's focus. Quickly surveying the image, Donna liked what she saw. "Six-one, one-eighty, jet black hair I could run my hands through for hours. Deep brown eyes, reminds me of that comedian in the cop movie that I rented." She listed, mentally. She smiled at Boo, wanting to make a good first impression. "Hello, can I help you?" she asked, sweetly.

"I hope so," Boo answered, and produced his copy of Kaycee Landing's book. "Do you know this woman?"

"Maybe…" This was going to be fun, Donna thought.

"I read this novel, and I can't get her out of my head. I know this probably sounds like some type of stalking, but I would truly like to meet her and talk to her. I think that I am in love with a woman that I've never met, and I was told that you are her friend. Can you help me and perhaps strike a blow for hopeless romantics everywhere?"

Donna looked Boo right in the eye, and replied, "Buddy, you just hit the jackpot."

Nine

"Hold on, Mack, you'll get your share, I promise. I won't forget you." Keith reassured the ball of fur working a manic figure eight around his legs. He half smiled and returned his gaze to the grill in front of him. He had ordered the freshest filet that the grocery had, and he was quite pleased when the kid delivered a hulking slab of lake trout. Keith lowered the heat and the lid and walked back to his chair on the deck. He chuckled when he realized that Mack hadn't followed, but was still staring intently at the grill, making sure that his master would share that delicious fish when it was ready to serve. The small television on the table was tuned to ESPN, and Keith was impatiently awaiting the update on this week's golf tournament. "Jeez, just give me the scores..." he pleaded to the screen. He enjoyed watching live golf, a fact that had amazed Mel. He remembered defending the sport by focusing on the solitary nature of it, how a good player could only depend on his own skill instead of teammates to get the job done. He also recalled her chiding him about it once, saying, "If the object of the game is to hit the ball the fewest number of times, then why play at all?" The logic of the statement slammed into his brain and he locked up for a few minutes, stammering and sputtering but never putting together a cohesive argument. She had laughed then, not at Keith but at the situation, and let him off the hook by kissing him on the forehead and telling him that if he enjoyed it, it must have merit. Keith smiled warmly at the memory, and recalled how much light and laughter that his wife had brought into their home. He was still thinking about Mel as his hand raised the beer to his mouth. He stopped when his lips touched the glass, and he stared at the bottle. "Never had this stuff in the fridge when you were here, hon." Keith said. "And you don't need it now, either", he imagined Mel's reply. He set the beer down on the table and stood to go check on his trout. Absent-mindedly, Keith almost stepped on Mack, who was still on guard in front of the grill and Mack let him know with a sharp meow. Happy with the look of their lunch, Keith shut off the grill and lifted the fish onto a platter, the ends of which extended to the length of the small table that sat on the deck. Keith pulled two chairs to the feast and called Mack to the table. He snickered as the tabby placed his front feet on the edge of the table and began to tear bite after bite from the trout. "At least I don't have to eat alone." Keith thought. About to taste his handiwork, Keith heard the sound of a vehicle in his driveway, and then the slam of a door and the rush of feet on gravel. "Always when I'm eating. God, Lannie, can't you give me more notice?" he said disgustedly, throwing his napkin onto the table and walking back into the house. By the time Keith reached the front door, Lannie was already inside. "What now?" he asked the obviously nervous woman.

"Hold on to your behind, Keith, or sit on it if you have to, but get ready, 'cause Kris Helton is about ten minutes behind me, and she's coming your way."

"Like Hell she is. What's going on, Lannie?" he asked, getting a crawly feeling on the back of his neck that told him that he already knew. His mood grew even blacker at the realization that very soon, chaos was going to set up camp in his cabin, and it would be planning to stay for a while.

"It's not my fault, Keith. She staked out my house and followed me when I left this morning. I tried to shake her, but she hung tight." Lannie gritted her teeth on the lie. She dearly hoped that Kris would be the impetus for Keith to climb out of his hole, and if she lost his trust in the process of his return to the human race, then so be it. "What are we going to do?" Lannie asked Keith.

"I'm going back to finish my lunch with Mack. You're going to tell Ms. Helton that if she doesn't leave quickly enough, you'll sic that sleazebag lawyer that the publisher uses on her, and every paycheck remaining in her workaday life will be sent directly to me." Keith whirled and started to climb. "And..." He was cut off by the creak of the front door opening again, and gaped at the sight of the face that belonged on the jacket of his book.

"I'm sorry, but the door was open. Hi, I'm Kris Helton, and I'm here to meet Kaycee Landing." She said, smiling from ear to ear. The elation that Kris was feeling was tremendous. The excitement over meeting the author that she had thought about nearly non-stop since the day that Donna saw the poster in the mall was almost overwhelming, and she was happy that she could stand without visibly shaking. That high, however, was short lived.

"There is no Kaycee Landing." Keith spat. "I made her up and used your picture, to which you have no rights. I don't know what you thought you would gain by coming here, but I assure you that it will be nothing. Leave now, before I throw you back to the city."

"Keith, that's not fair. You at least owe her an explanation, don't you think?" Lannie asked, hoping to stall to plan.

"No, I don't." Keith replied flatly. A small part of him, however, was feeling a bit of admiration for Kris. Even the most persistent of his fans hadn't gotten this close, and this woman didn't even know whom Keith was. She was looking for the woman that wrote <u>A Love Worth Living</u>, not a bleak, cynical curmudgeon, and in the instant that his rational mind admitted this fact, it stumbled upon the notion that there might be something worthwhile inside of her. Something that Keith hadn't seen in a long, long time.

"What did you say? I'm sorry, but I'm confused. You made up whom?" Kris asked, face scrunched and eyes pleading. Her brain was trying to process what it thought that it heard, and her body felt like someone had punched her deep in the stomach, knocking the wind from her. Her eyes flashed quickly to Lannie, then to Keith and back, hoping that someone would help her understand what had just occurred. Unfortunately, Keith spoke first.

"Kaycee Landing does not exist. I wrote the book. If that isn't enough information for you, then I suggest you ask Ms. Reyes there. She seems to have taken an interest in you, but God knows why." Keith shot a cold, raw look at Lannie, and then mounted the stairs. Without turning, he continued, "I am resuming my lunch now. I would hope that both of you are gone when I am finished." With that said, he left the room.

Kris was aghast. Her dream had been quickly reversed and was approaching nightmare conditions, and worse, she had no idea what her next move should be. She faced Lannie, correctly figuring her as an ally, and tried to speak. All that her swimming mind could push out was one word: "What?"

"I'm sorry, Kris, I really am." Lannie began. She felt badly for Kris, and was frantically searching her thoughts for a way to ease a little of Kris' consternation. "Listen, have you ever heard of an author by the name of Keith Randall? Real recluse, best seller?" she asked.

Kris shook her head, clearing the cobwebs. "Yeah, some kind of weirdo who is never seen in public. He writes those really dark crime novels, right?"

"That's right. Well guess what, hon, you just met him." Lannie watched as her words washed over Kris like warm water, and smiled wistfully as her eyes widened with revelation.

"How could someone like him write something that is so beautiful? It brought me to tears more than once, but I just met him and all I feel for him is contempt. I can't believe that those words came from that man." Kris scowled, pointing animatedly toward the stairwell. "Explain that contradiction to me, Ms. Reyes, please."

"First, it's Lannie. There's no use in being formal here. Secondly, I realize that it seems completely incongruous with his past style, and with the display that you witnessed, but I assure you that Keith did write that book, using a part of him that he doesn't allow to surface very often. That story is Keith's. The love was between him and Mel, his wife. Keith started writing after she died, and like you said, his stuff was, is, very dark and dreary. From the little that I've been able to gather, Mel was his light, his way out of a terribly lonely existence. I'm hoping that he can be redeemed, because if he doesn't make a turn, he's going to die. Maybe not physically, but most certainly spiritually, and I'm also hoping that you'll help me."

"With what, Lannie?" Kris asked, not quite sure where Lannie was going with this speech.

"Keith picked that picture of you for a reason, Kris, a reason that I'm not sure he even knows. He told me that he felt Mel's presence the entire time that he was working on the book, and that as soon as the manuscript left his hand, he lost that feeling." Lannie paused to gauge the mood in Kris' eyes. "He needs to care again, Kris. And he needs to know that someone cares about him. Maybe then he can find Mel once more, and find some semblance of wholeness." A plan had finally been articulated, and Lannie was astonished at the depth of belief she had in the words that had left her mouth. A stand had to be made, but she realized now that she would never have been able to do it alone. She prayed that Kris would agree to stay. "What do you say?"

Kris stared at Lannie for what seemed like an eternity. Then she dropped her purse and plopped into an easy chair. "Tell me more, Lannie," she sighed, "tell me more."

About half of the trout was missing when Keith got back to the deck, and a suspiciously bloated tabby cat was lounging under the table, purring contentedly. The remaining share was only lukewarm, and Keith decided to return it to the fire for re-heating. Standing in front of the grill, his mind raced. He was starting to consider Lannie a friend, something he hadn't done in a month of Sundays, and had even been enjoying the visits she made infrequently to his home, but this episode with Kris was infuriating. He felt betrayed by Lannie, and he knew that she had some level of complicity in Kris' arrival at the cabin. On the other hand, he hadn't tried to sound as ugly as he had toward Kris, but the blackness of his character had a way of rearing up unabated and fierce when unchecked, and since Mel, all the stops were pulled. A familiar smell brought Keith out of his introspection, and he pulled his lunch from the fire quickly enough to prevent a total loss. As he trudged toward the table, Mack perked up and spoke. "You've had quite enough, Mack attack, no more for you." Keith replied to the cat. A thin grin followed the first bite of trout, and then a cheer toward the television. ESPN had just given the scores that Keith had been waiting for, and two of his favorites were on the top of the leaderboard. Suddenly, another memory of his former life came rushing into his mind, and again, he could hear Mel's voice floating through his head. "If I'd known that you liked the game that much, we would've bought the other plots out back and you could have built your own course. Oh well, 'C'est la vie' babe." He laughed as he remembered his reply to Mel's statement. He had told her that it was just as well, because he would've ended up closing the place to the public, and continuing with a private club of one. Polishing off the rest of his food, Keith began to think harder about the past few days. He slowly realized that he was reminiscing more and more about Mel again, as if fate had removed a gate from the pathways of his mind. He reached down to the floor and hoisted Mack to his lap, scratching behind his ears. "You know, Mack Daddy, I was a better person before you came here. Not that it's your fault that I'm a jerk. I wonder if I'll ever know how much of me was scattered to the winds along with her ashes. Anything that was good in me was from her, and I threw myself into a big, black hole after she died. I guess I finally realized that I missed that part of me, and that's why I wrote the romance. I needed to feel that again, and the only way that I could think of was to write about Mel. You only get one chance to love like that Mack. Only one."

"You're right, but it doesn't mean that you quit trying."

"How long have you been there, Lannie?"

"Long enough to wish that I had known your wife. Keith, you need help. Please let me. Kris too, and even after I had told her all the info that I know about you. She's a good kid, Keith, and she came all this way to talk to the person that wrote that book. She wants to know about the love that you wrote about, and frankly, so do I. And maybe talking about it will help you rediscover it. C'mon down Keith. Please."

Ten

"Gimme your heart, make it real or else forget about it... hmm mmm mmm" Boo sang along to the song on the radio. He had a vague idea of his destination, and was somewhat sure that he was on the right road. Less certain though, was his plan once he met Kaycee. Her friend Donna had told him that she was in close contact with Kaycee during her trip and that she was going to a small town up north. Boo popped another McNugget into his mouth and thought hard about his first move. Even though it wasn't his nature to, he wanted to be sure not to come on too strong. He also didn't want to appear like a crazed fan, either; so a cautious level of enthusiasm mixed with respect and a liberal dose of his natural, "aw shucks" demeanor would have to be the correct recipe. As the road stretched along the wooded wilderness, Boo kept thinking about the foolish aspects of what he was doing. He'd been in relationships before, and was sure that he was in love with Anne for a time, but nothing had felt the same as this. Truthfully, it was odd to be altering your world for a person that you think you know by reading the words that they have put to paper, but it wasn't any stranger than love's normal modus operandi. All that Boo was looking for was an audience with a woman that had touched his soul, and perhaps the chance to share a little life with her. He reached his right hand out and noticed that his food was gone, and decided to pull to the shoulder for another glimpse at the road map. Using his finger to make the mile scale, his estimated that he had about an hour left to the town that Donna had mentioned by name just before she left earshot. "Go get her, Boo!" he remembered Donna yelling. He carefully refolded the map and eased his beast back onto the highway, then reached into his shirt and grasped St. Christopher, wishing with all his might that this weekend would be one that he would never forget. "Man, I should get out of Ann Arbor more often. It's really beautiful up here." He thought aloud. The early afternoon sun played hide-and-seek with him as he passed clumps of roadside trees, and his open window allowed him to hear the birds and crickets working on symphony after unfinished symphony. An open field next to a curve in the road gave Boo his first-ever deer sighting, a pair of yearlings frolicking with each other through the tall grass. He was almost ready to believe that he had passed into another time, one much quainter and precious than his own and then the manure truck pulled out in front of him. The stench was nearly unbearable, and unfortunately for Boo, he had reached a place in the road marked by signs reading, "No Passing Next 15 Miles". Instantly, his mind flashed, "Welcome to the northland, Boo. Hope you survive the visit."

Lannie stood behind the recliner in the living room and tried to survey the situation. On her mental list of good signs was the fact that Keith had actually come back downstairs. Canceling that out on the bad sign list, however, was that his first action upon leaving the stairwell was to walk to the refrigerator and grab a beer. She turned her head and saw Mack sitting in Kris' lap, potentially a good sign. The tabby was competing for attention with Kris' cell-phone, though, and that was probably a bad sign. Keith had now moved through the kitchen to the far end of the living room, away from the rest of the guests, and had begun to rifle through his CD collection. Lannie could hear him muttering faintly, but she wasn't sure if it was due to the situation with Kris or just the fact that he wasn't finding the disc he had his heart set upon. Kris broke the silence first.

"Hey Lannie, did you know that Mack here likes to talk on the phone? I put it near his ear and he meowed every time that Donna asked him a question. Amazing, eh?" Mack looked up as if he knew exactly what Kris had said and meowed once more.

"Sure, disturb my house and then corrupt my cat." Keith said dryly. He had sauntered over and joined Lannie and Kris, at least physically. Lannie was hoping that Keith would not begin another tirade, and to her relief, he didn't. In fact, he put down his beer and looked directly at Kris and Lannie. With steel in his eyes, he asked, "All right, Lannie says that I need help. Who are you two to provide it?"

"A fair question, and one that deserves an answer." Lannie replied. "I think that I know you as well as anyone, and I care about you. You are driving yourself into a self-destructive state from which you will not emerge if you don't stop now. There are still worthwhile things in you, Keith, you just need to realize it."

Kris continued in the same vein. "The man that wrote this book is obviously the man that Mel fell in love with, the man that she chose to spend the rest of her life with. Don't tell me that you can easily sweep him away like yesterday's dust."

Keith chuckled humorlessly. "You've nailed it exactly, my dear Kris. 'Yesterdays'. That's all they are.

Mel died once, then I resurrected her for this damn book and she died again. Are you suggesting that I keep this cycle of abuse going? Maybe next time I can write a novel based on what I felt the moment that cop told me about the accident. God knows that it's never far from my mind." He was almost ranting now, but alongside the anger in his eyes, Kris thought that she also saw some of the pain that rose from the wound in Keith's soul. She glanced over at Lannie, who, on the verge of tears, seemed ready to bolt across the room and grab Keith in a never-ending embrace. She loves him, Kris thought, I just wonder how much. She opened her mouth to interject, but was cut off by Keith. "Perhaps I enjoy this solitary existence. Being the bastard that I am, what makes you ladies think that I would want to change?" Keith punctuated his question with a nasty grin, feeling that he had gained a slight foothold over his opponents. He waited for Kris to answer, and then flashed to Lannie, who was now unable to contain the water that had been welling behind her eyelids. Tears streaming, Lannie stepped toward Keith and with quiet conviction said two words to him. "The book."

"The book..." Keith repeated. He let the words fall once more from his lips and then looked away from the women. Why did everything keep coming back to the book? And why when it was mentioned, did Keith feel the blood drain from his face? Because you keep coming back to me, Keith imagined Mel saying. He raised his face, realizing that not only were Lannie and Kris crying, but he was too. Without words, he shuffled over to the stereo and shut it down, enveloping the cabin in only the sounds of sorrow. Lannie looked at Keith as he slumped against the wall with a strange look of grace on her face. She believed that she had just witnessed another human being experience an epiphany, and she swore that she could see a door, long barred shut, opening once more in the soul of Keith Randall. She stood, wanting to reach him and hold his head in her hands, wanting to whisper into his ear and make him believe in the moment, but another hand brushed hers and made her pause. "No." said Kris softly and shaking her head. "Let him find this on his

own. He has to touch her, and he can't if you're there."
Lannie looked at Kris, a part of her wanting to scream
filthy things toward the interloper, but the bigger part
knowing that each word Kris had said was true.
Unfortunately, knowing this also broke her heart.

"I had pretty much decided to spend the rest of my
life alone, you know," Keith began in a tear-stained
voice. "In college, I mean. I had no use for anyone, and
really didn't care if anybody wanted to get to know me.
The day that Mel introduced herself to me on the
concourse was a true turning point. As she spoke, I
could feel things break inside of me. Stubborn things,
dark and angry ones. She was my opposite number, the
yin to my yang, so to speak. I swear that I could see
straight to her soul just by looking into her eyes. My
grandmother used to say that there is a lid for every
pot, and Mel covered me completely." Calmness had
settled into Keith's face, and his body seemed to loosen.
"Even though I tried to fight against it, there was no
doubt that I was in love with her. In an instant, I knew
that this woman was the only chance I would ever have
to save myself from the road that I was traveling, and I

grabbed it." Keith smiled wistfully, as he pictured Mel with her tousled, streaky hair and her too large boxer shorts. "And luckily, Mel grabbed back." Keith stood, more to stretch than for any other reason, and as he did, a knock came to the door of the cabin. The sudden noise caused both Lannie and Kris to jump, and sent Mack sailing upstairs. Somewhat confused, and mostly irritated, Keith strode to the door and opened it, coming face to face with a rather sheepish looking young man.

Keith turned toward the women only to be met with unknowing stares and shrugged shoulders. He was about to ask the uninvited exactly what he thought he was doing there, but the man beat him to the punch. "Umm… Hi, my name is Boone Arloe, and I realize that this is going to sound very odd, but is Kaycee Landing here? A friend of hers told me that I might find her in this neighborhood, so did I come to the right place?" Boo asked, trying to look as sincere as he hoped he sounded. Keith processed this information, and two options raised themselves in his mind. One, he could slam the door in Boo's face after an expletive-laced tirade, or two, he could throw a little of this current

122

chaos in somebody else's lap. With a grin on his face, he chose number two.

"Well Mr. Arloe, you've come to the right place." Keith said, and he pointed toward Kris sitting in the living room. "There she is, the beautiful and talented Kaycee Landing."

Eleven

Half an hour had passed since Boo entered the cabin, and he was standing in the living room alone. Seconds after Keith had pointed in Kris' direction; she had bolted for the safety of the kitchen. Lannie followed her, and then Lannie returned and dragged Keith away with her. Boo knew that something - or someone - more likely, was being discussed loudly, but he couldn't make out the actual words, which was probably a good thing.

"What the hell was that little operation, Keith?" an incredulous Kris demanded.

"The guy is looking for you, 'Kaycee', I just helped him along." Keith replied, still quite pleased. He was about to pat himself on the back again when Lannie interjected.

"You know, Keith, I'm sure that he came looking for Kris' face, but he's also looking for your words. Don't forget that you've created a composite human being here, and if you don't want the entire thing to go up in flames, the two of you are going to have to play this out to the end." Lannie paused and waited for the arguments that she was sure were coming. In the moment that Boo stepped through the door, Lannie scrapped the original plan and began thinking on her feet. The only way, she surmised, to get Keith to re-establish his link with himself and his memories of Mel was to get him to re-live them. What better way, she thought, than to teach Kris how to be Kaycee Landing? By doing this, as Kris became Kaycee, Keith would then hopefully become the man with whom Mel fell in love. Unfortunately, Boo Arloe might become the innocent victim of a drive-by rebirth. "This needs to work, you two, and you need to figure out how to do it. I'll go out there and entertain Mr. Arloe. Join us when you're prepared."

Watching Lannie saunter through the door, Keith glared at Kris. "You've read the book?"

"Devoured it. Felt every word. You're a bastard, but a truly talented one." Kris replied. She grinned slightly and saw that she had elicited the same from Keith. He had warmed slightly since Kris arrived, and he actually was starting to see Kris in a different light. She was a strong woman, and she held to her opinions hard and fast. Maybe, somehow, Keith had been able to glimpse that inner character in just a simple photograph and that was why Kris reminded him so much of Mel. "Now let me ask you something, okay?" Kris began. "The story is yours and Mel's, I know that much, you just reversed the gender roles. What I need to know, though, is who Kaycee Landing really is."

"She has my voice, Kris, my words," Keith answered. "But in my mind she definitely wore Mel's face. When the time came to title the book, I just couldn't bear to put her name and face on it. I guess that's why I picked your photo. You looked so vital and strong, and that's how Mel was every day of her life. It just fit."

Kris felt instantly flattered by the comparison to Keith's wife, and suddenly realized that even if the rest of the world saw Keith as a jerk; Mel truly loved him with everything that she was. "I should apologize for the 'bastard' remark. It was uncalled for." Kris said, and tried to shift the focus back to Keith, and away from the memories that she feared she might be inspiring. Keith grinned thinly again, and waved his hand toward Kris.

"No need. I am a bastard most of the time. You just seem to call them as you see them." Quiet returned to the kitchen, then, albeit not an altogether uncomfortable one. Kris was sitting on the island in the middle of the room, dangling her feet and swaying them from left to right. Her gaze flitted around, landing on Keith, then the glass doors of the cupboards. Keith shifted his weight from one foot to the other, but did not raise his head to look or speak.

"I wouldn't pick you to be a Cocoa Pebbles fan, Keith. I see a couple of boxes in the cupboard over there. Any other culinary secrets hanging about?" Kris asked. She was merely trying to break the mild tension, but her query did get Keith talking again.

"Not really..." was the reply.

"Come on, I'll bet you drink Tang, too." Kris joked.

"Actually, it's very strange. Mel ate a bowl of that crap every morning for breakfast, along with a big glass of chocolate milk. Since she... passed, I still order a box from the grocer, although it eventually is thrown to the birds out back. They also seem to like it."

"Keith?"

"Hmm? What, Kris?" Keith looked at her intently, as if waiting for her to make a grand statement then leap from the island into the air. Instead, she leaned in toward him.

"Please tell me about you. How you felt when Mel was alive. How you fell for her, and what it was like when you realized that you were really, truly in love. I want to know, no, I need to know." Kris' voice was nearly pleading. "Because if I'm going to be Kaycee Landing, we need to face the facts: I need to be you."

Lannie was sitting in a recliner, stroking Mack's fur, and watching Boo run his fingers through Keith's compact discs. He was cute, in a free-spirit sort of way, Lannie thought, and it showed true determination and spunk to track down Chateau Randall. He also seemed quite genuine to Lannie, and there was definitely an air of wonder around Mr. Arloe when he set eyes upon Kris. "See anything you like, Mr. Arloe?" Lannie asked, trying to lead Boo into conversation.

"Please, it's Boo, and as far as the CD's go, this is one eclectic collection. I mean, he has the Refreshments and W.C. Handey and Jeff Buckley, and then there's Nina Simone and Prince. Very 'across-the-board'. And Mo'Zella? Who is she?"

"Detroiter..." Lannie answered off-handedly. "Keith says that she's very good. Anyway, you didn't really answer my question." Lannie smiled.

"You're referring to Ms. Landing, eh? Well, to be honest, she is as beautiful as I had hoped when I hatched this plan. I really believe that I felt a connection with her when I read her book. The love that courses through those lines is the type that we all aspire to find, and I would simply like the opportunity to meet the source of the story." Boo concluded, feeling that he had stated his case as well as was possible. "Truthfully, though, I didn't really expect to stumble into some sort of writer's enclave. I mean, I'll feel very stupid if there is something between Kaycee and Mr. Randall."

Lannie was surprised, and felt as though she was about to fall out of the chair. "You know who Keith is?" she asked.

"Sure. I review books for a semi-living at the university, and I've read his last two for my column. I must admit, in person he looks just as grumpy as the picture on his last novel."

"Where he's flipping off the photographer..." Lannie laughed, replaying the entire photo session in her head. Boo was certainly no dummy, she thought, but he doesn't have a fix on what he's discovered yet. She hoped, for the sake of everyone in the cabin that the upcoming charade would come off without a hitch.

"You went to U of M to study ancient civilizations? Who the hell does that?" The incredulous look on Kris' face only served to underscore the bewilderment in her question. Keith had agreed to tell her about Mel, but he began with college. Even with Kris prodding him, he refused to speak about anything dealing with his childhood. "I mean, how were you ever going to use those skills later in life? I can just see you at the quad, thinking 'Hmm, I could echo the Phoenicians and just get the salad or maybe the Incas and sacrifice the sous chef.'"

"Well," Keith explained, "my driving force in life was to be alone. What better way than by becoming an anthropologist and losing myself in some pyramid or ruin somewhere? To me, it seemed perfect." Self-consciously, Keith realized that he was grinning again. He looked at her, still seated on the island, still swinging her legs, and saw a person who had truly cared about the people in that book. Therefore, she truly cared about Mel and Keith, and to Keith, that was both comforting and unsettling at the same time. "Okay, my turn. What would possess someone to paint her toenails a shade of pink whose closest analog in nature would be a sunburned flamingo?"

Kris looked down at her now naked feet. She had absent-mindedly kicked off her sneakers after achieving her butcher-block perch, and was unaware that by doing so she would be required to defend her use of a polish aptly named "House of Whores". "Fine, I admit it, not a great choice, but I'm not in the habit of showing my feet to just anyone, you know. But you, my surly friend, are getting off-subject."

Keith huffed sternly at Kris, and then continued. "Of course you know how I met Mel, but there was another episode a day later that, in retrospect, seems much more telling of the events to come." He gazed at the ceiling, as if trying to see through it to the past. He remembered waking to a phone call from the campus bookstore manager alerting him to a shipment of new Greco-Roman pottery guides. To an anthropology student, this was an event on par with free beer night at the Blind Pig. He threw on his clothes from the previous day and made the trek across campus. Cursing the unseasonably cold wind that morning, Keith was caught, mid-mutter, by a now familiar voice. "Keith! How come you're here so early, buddy?" Mel had asked him, and for the first time in years, Keith was actually excited to see another human being. He told Mel what he was there for, and she surprised him with a semi-interest in his particular reading material. Mel was always looking at technique when it came to art, and the use of urns as canvas for storytelling was intriguing. The two of them talked for half an hour after the bookstore opened, but then class was calling Mel, and she took her leave. Grasping at straws, Keith threw a comment to her about having more such books at his apartment, and she would be welcome to stop by, anytime. This was another first for Keith, as he had never invited anyone into his home. Making matters even more alarmingly odd was the fact that Mel, smiling over her shoulder, yelled back that she would. So thrilled at the prospect of enjoying more time with Mel, Keith completely forgot about the textbook and ran back to his apartment to plan out the perfect impression to give to Mel.

"Do you think they've run off, left us to fend for ourselves?" Boo asked Lannie. He was now pacing nervously back and forth in front of Lannie's chair, and was in serious danger of making Mack dizzy. "I mean, it's been almost an hour since they went into the kitchen. What could they be doing?"

After an agitated Mack left her lap, Lannie stood and put a hand on Boo's shoulder. He stopped and she looked sweetly into his eyes. "Don't worry about them, sport. Trust me, there is nothing going on romantically between Keith and Kaycee. Now, is there some sort of base, physical notion that set you on the northern trail? Not trying to sound old-fashioned, but are your intentions honorable with Ms. Landing? I don't believe that you've really made things clear, Boo."

Although Lannie's smile and demeanor were calming, Boo still felt that he was under interrogation. To be fair, Lannie was right; he hadn't made any declarations yet. "I'm sorry, Lannie. I guess I'm trying my best not to appear as a psycho. I just felt that my fate was tied to finding the woman that wrote that book." Boo paused, then added, "But, saying it out loud, it does make me seem a bit touched..."

Keith thought for sure that he was going to have to pick Kris from off the floor after she finished the laughing jag that she was currently enjoying. There wasn't much in his history that Keith thought would be this hilarious. The story had gotten through Mel's first visit, the broken finger he'd incurred trying to keep a large clay pot from hitting Mel in the head, three other "dates" and graduation. He had just begun to talk about the cabin when Kris started guffawing. "What's so damned funny?" he finally asked.

"Hee hee, only the fact that your wife fell for probably the most anal man in the history of anal...ness." Kris replied, sniffling. Keith grinned slightly. Mel referred to him as "anal" quite often, but admitted that that quality was a perfect compliment to her free spirit. "Don't you see Keith? You two were meant for each other. God's will, fate, kismet, call it what you want, but you can't deny that."

"I suppose her death was fate, too, hmm?" Keith was cold again, and Kris realized that she had just snapped the tightrope linking Keith to the rest of humanity. "The book basically covers everything else, so you should have no problem impersonating the author. I'm done with this, and I'm going back upstairs."

"Dammit Keith! You need to start living again. Stop trying to scatter yourself after those ashes in the yard." Kris leapt from the island and ran after Keith, who was already in the stairwell. She grabbed for his hand but was surprised when he whirled and slapped it away. All that she could see in him was ice.

"Don't you even dare to tell me how to live. When you love someone to those depths and lose them, we'll talk. Until then, just leave me and my memories alone!" Keith continued on his way, leaving a tearful Kris in his wake.

Stunned, and unable to argue with an empty room, Kris let go a deep breath. Vacations weren't supposed to give a person so much grief. She put the back of her hand to her eyes to catch the drops, not crying for herself, but for the two people who had created such joy in this home years ago.

Twelve

"There's my girl!" Lannie said as Kris came into the room from the kitchen. She hoped that Kris was ready to continue the subterfuge, but the red eyes and nose that Kris was sporting seemed to contradict that theory. The younger woman shuffled toward one of the overstuffed chairs opposite Lannie and Boo, and slumped down. Her body language hinted slightly at defeat, and Lannie could now tell that Kris had been crying. She leaned forward, trying to telepathically ask Kris what had happened, only to be rebuked with a small hand wave. Well, Lannie thought, this is what I'm good at, so here goes. "Kaycee, while you and Keith were in the other room, Mr. Arloe and I..."

"Boo, please, Lannie. Just Boo."

"...Boo and I spoke about his quest, and I don't think that you really need to worry about him. I do feel that he just wants to learn a little about love."

"I think we could all learn a little about love, Lannie." Kris replied, rolling her eyes toward the ceiling. Instantly, Lannie was on the same page as her, and could sympathize with the resignation in Kris' voice. "So, Boo... what exactly can I do for you? Or is that much too loaded of a question to send your way?"

A shy grin played its way across Boo's face before he answered; intimating that he'd indeed had one or two baser thoughts about the object of his affection. "I suppose that a grander statement is in order, but I would be honored to be able to get to know you. Your face on the jacket caused me to pick up a book that I normally would have dismissed as trivial and undeserving. As I read, I could imagine the words flowing from your mouth, and I felt a connection forging with you, one that I had to examine to its fullest potential. I went to the publisher first, and then a friend of mine at a bookstore told me that you had recently surprised them with a visit. She helped me track down your friend Donna, who in turn helped to this cabin. I don't normally believe in destiny, but it seems almost karmic the way things fell together, and I think that I deserve a chance. Who knows? Everything happens for a reason, and well... here I am." Boo was almost out of breath, and was sure that he could have been more eloquent, but decided to rest his case.

"Wow. You know, Boo, just because I'm an author it doesn't mean that you have to unload every ten-dollar word that you have in your head. Trust me, I'm not one to be plowed under with the horseshit. Just admit that you're currently visualizing the style and color of my panties, and how quickly they can be removed." With an evil gleam in her eyes, Kris sat back in her chair and watched, as Boone Arloe became a quivering, self-conscious mess.

"But, no… you, you've got it all wrong. I… I mean, you've got me wrong. Getting to know you, that's what I had planned."

"In the Biblical sense? Please. I have something to attend to upstairs. Maybe you'll have a clearer picture of said plans when I return."

Lannie stepped out of the way and covered her mouth to stifle a laugh as Kris pushed through the kitchen door. "Ouch. Score one for the lady…" she whispered. Kris put a finger to her lips and flashed a quick grin, then continued up the stairs. Lannie had to wonder about Kris, though. How long could she keep pretending? Boone didn't seem to be some local yokel to be snowed and sent on his merry way. Surely, he could crack this little formula that Lannie had concocted if given enough time. Besides, he was starting to cross from earnest and cute to entitled and insufferable. She wished that Keith would come down the stairs and kick Mr. Arloe square in his skinny ass. "We'll be lucky if he hasn't thrown himself off of the balcony by now. He can't be well with all this chaos in his home."

Keith stood on his deck, staring out into the purpling sky. Twilight was at hand, Mel's favorite time of the evening. The color of the sky foretold more rain, probably a thunderstorm. Quickly, Keith turned around to check the window, and then smiled when a certain tabby returned his gaze. "Can't have you wandering out in a storm, Mack. I need you right where you are." What he needed the most right now, though, were answers. Keith actually felt bad, no; make that awful, for snapping at Kris. What was worse were the facts that he wanted her to know more about Mel, and he wanted to know more about Kris, and that scared him, as evidenced by the goose bumps. Even once you were past the physical, there was a lot about Kris that reminded him of Mel. She made him laugh in spite of himself, and that was no mean feat. Kris had an easy way about her, a vibe that allowed another human being to just "be" when they were in her company. Keith's relationship with Lannie was a bit more than the standard "client/agent" ideal, but not what anyone would classify as close. He would banter with her if he were feeling mischievous, but other than rage or disgust, there weren't many emotions that he shared with her. Kris, however... he wanted Kris to know-

"Hey?"

He whirled, shocked, and hoping that the gasp that he caught in his throat hadn't been audible. He wasn't sure what he looked like when he faced Kris, but he prayed that she couldn't see the fear in his eyes.

"Did you deal with Mr. Arloe?" he asked, trying to stay in control of the situation. He had no idea that the constant crossing and uncrossing of his arms was proof that control had quickly deserted Keith at the first sign of trouble.

"I was rude and snide to him. I figured that I'd be you. In fact, I may have made him cry. I'm not sure; I didn't stay long enough to find out."

"Heh. That's funny. I..."

"Enough, Keith. I have had enough. I saw the look on your face when you turned around. I know that you can't keep that shell up all the time. And I damn sure know that I am not going to let you destroy all that you and Mel built, just because you can't find the strength to leave your personal pity party."

"Don't you come up here and lecture me! You've no idea…"

Thunder from a storm down on the lake rumbled faintly, and the glow of heat lightning turned the violet horizon briefly to red. Kris then took advantage of the pregnant pause that Mother Nature had given her.

"Wrong. Wrong, wrong, wrong. You keep repeating that, but it isn't true. I have every idea, because you put it all down on paper. I wish that I had loved someone as much as you loved Mel, and I'm sorry that you lost her, truly I am. But is this any way to honor her? By becoming a horrible human being?" Tears began to fill Kris' eyes, and she held herself tight to keep from crying. "Is it?'

"I honored her with the book! I told her story!"

Now Kris was angry. "No, you told your story, the both of you. You may hate me for saying this, but Mel wasn't some saint. She was a human being looking for another and found you. All she did was help you become who you really wanted to be. Now you've decided to piss on everything she gave you and fall back into being the sorry asshole that hides what Mel loved. I hope that you're fucking happy with that decision, because I guarantee that she wouldn't be!"

Stunned, Keith stared at the tornado that was spinning away, with the fact that he didn't know what to do next smacking him in the forehead like a boxer on greenies working a speed bag. "Kris, stop! There's a storm blowing in, a bad one. I don't want you upset and traveling."

She was still seething. "Where would you like me, then?"

In my arms, said a small voice in the back of Keith's brain. He shook his head to remove the offending thought. Where the Hell did that come from, he thought. He moved toward Kris, hoping that he wouldn't be slapped upon entering her personal space. "Amazingly, Mel suggested that we build this place large enough to entertain company, so there's plenty of space for you to bunk here tonight. I normally sleep in the den, downstairs, so if you'd like, you can use this bedroom."

The anger drained from Kris and was instantly replaced with confusion. She'd be damned, however, if she would let Keith in on that secret. "Fine. I don't like driving in the rain anyway. I'll just go get my bag, and then in the morning, I'll get out of Dodge." She spun and continued through the door, exasperated but strangely... intrigued. Did Keith hope to gain something from having her stay, or was it just basic human concern? The only thing that he knew for sure was that it had been one Hell of a day, one that he had no inclination of ever repeating.

"Tell Lannie and Mr. Arloe to also pick a room," Keith yelled after her. "There will be no accidents that in any way can be blamed on me tonight!"

Thirteen

The storm that arrived was indeed a doozy. In fact, the first peal of lightning sent Mack rushing into the master bedroom with his hind end almost ahead of his front. Kris had gotten to her car for her bag, and was lucky enough to only be half-drenched upon returning to the cabin. Keith informed his guests of the basic layout of the cabin, warned them of midnight visits from Mack, then promptly retired to the den, with an insincere "sleep well" trailing in his wake. Boo was still trying to plead his case to Kris, who was having nothing to do with him. Lannie was staring daggers at Kris after finding out that the master bedroom had been given to her for the night, even though Kris swore that she had nothing to do with the decision.

"What is the problem, Lannie? First, you're my buddy, now you're pissed off?"

"I don't see the need for you to be sleeping in that bed… room. There are three guest bedrooms on this level. And I'm not pissed. I just think that you could be a better guest." Lannie crossed her arms and set her jaw, attaining a posture that was normally construed as "Take that, bitch." With her mouth open and shaking her head, Kris left the living room.

"Nothing at all going on between them, huh?" Boo had knelt next to the chair that Lannie was sitting in, and was going to enjoy the needling that he planned to deliver. There was something not right going on in this cabin, and Boo knew that he had to get everyone's allegiances in order before the night was through. Lannie obviously had feelings for Keith, anyone could see that, but Kaycee and Keith were a different matter.

148

Certainly there was a gulf between the two of them, but Boo couldn't pin it down. There were sparks in their conversations, but just as much ice followed them. If there wasn't anything romantic occurring with these two now, it wouldn't be long before there was, Boo surmised. "So, why the drama about the bedroom? Have you been there before?" Even though he was kneeling next to her, Boo could feel the heat coming from Lannie's cheeks. Yes, he smiled, I have her.

"Asshole! What makes you think that you can ask me something like that?" Lannie folded her arms and pouted, trying very hard not to let Boo know that he'd struck a nerve. Of course, it was too late.

"C'mon Lannie, it's easy to see how you pine for the man. I'm just trying to figure things out. Did you two have something, but now little miss author has entered the scene? I guess that I can understand wanting to be with one of your own, so to..." The last word caught in Boo's throat as Lannie whirled to face him.

"How dense can you be?" she hissed. "She's no more an author than Mack over there is a tiger. Keith wrote the book. For his wife. His dead wife. That's why the book is so fucking good. He wrote about what they had, and what he lost. He didn't want his name on the book, so he created an author and found a picture to go with the name. Ms. Landing is really a young woman named Kris Helton who coincidentally saw her picture in the promo material for the book's release. She tracked me down, followed me here, and you showed up later. Need anything else spelled out for you, ace?"

Boo was mouth-hanging open agog at what Lannie had said. None of it made sense to him, and hearing it was sending his plans crashing down around him. He turned slowly as he stood. "No... Kaycee Landing, just some girl. A romance by a thriller writer. And I'm a fool." He'd made it to the refrigerator and had pulled a couple of local pale ales from the door. He trudged back over to Lannie and sat once more on the floor next to her, handing one of the bottles to her, which she readily accepted.

"No more a fool than I am, dear Boo. I allowed Kris to follow me here, I guess in hope that she would kick Keith out of his self-destructive stupor. What I failed to realize was how much my devotion to Keith as a client had turned into love for him as a person." She took a pull of the ale, sighing contentedly as it rolled down to her stomach. "And now, I'm pissed because I'm afraid that he's going to fall for the woman that I delivered to his doorstep."

"At least you know how you feel about him. What the hell is my next move? I've fallen for a ghost, and I suspect, so has Kris."

Lannie nodded. "You're right, and so did I. We all have been following ghosts, Boo. Every last one of us." Lannie slid out of the chair and stretched, her sweater riding up on the curve of her breasts and revealing her navel to Boo. He opened his eyes a little wider, realizing how pretty Lannie was. She had a woman's body, full and curvy, but not heavy, not in the least. Her stomach was flat and she had "points all her own, sittin' way up high" as the song said. Her face was lived-in, but smooth, and she had the easy smile of everyone's best friend. Suddenly, he hated to see her feeling like this. He handed her his beer and scuttled over to the stereo, setting it low so only the two of them could hear the soft, slow music. Boo kind of waltzed back to Lannie, taking both of the bottles in one hand, and Lannie's hand in the other.

"I'm sorry if I insulted you, it truly wasn't my intent. I'm the one that's late to the party, and I was simply trying to catch up. Honestly, though, I didn't expect the bomb that you dropped on me."

"I'm not insulted, really. In fact, I think that spilling all this to you has helped me discover some things." Lannie hoped that she wasn't blushing; that hopefully the heat in her face was from the fire that Keith had built before going to bed. She looked Boo in the eyes though, and didn't turn. "Truthfully, though, I didn't plan to drop it. I was... I am furious at our 'friends' at the opposite ends of the hall here. I guess that I wanted the whole thing to come crashing down; misery loves company and all that." She shook her head, trying to clear her own cobwebs. Maybe she'd broken a dream that she should never have had, but if she really cared about Keith, it didn't matter who helped him get better, just that he did. Lannie still had Boo's hand in hers, and was slowly guiding him to the couch. He wasn't boorish and insufferable now, she thought, but sweet and unfortunately, just as lonely as Lannie. "Now that you know, however, I have no choice. I'll have to-"

"Have to kill me?" Boo grinned, as he felt his legs bump against the sofa.

Playfully, Lannie looked at Boo and smiled slyly. "Well, there are less drastic ways to keep you from talking, right?"

The master bedroom was beautiful, and it didn't have the basic look that the rest of the cabin had; Keith kept this room pristine. No dust was on the furniture, and the linens smelled of fresh air. Even though she felt a little creepy doing it, Kris couldn't completely suppress her innate curiosity and had started to poke around the master bedroom. Not maliciously, mind you, but just to try to make sense of what was happening. It was maddening to watch Keith's Jekyll and Hyde act, and even though both Lannie and Keith had given her the back story, she was convinced there was more that she needed to know. She opened the closet, looking for an extra blanket then noticed a half-door on the opposite wall of the walk-in. The tarnished knob turned easily, and within was a small trunk. "In for a penny, in for a pound..." she muttered. Upon lifting the lid, her gaze was drawn to an ornate book jacket. She pulled the book from its crèche, and then sat down on the floor. Kris had in her hands Keith's college yearbook, but the loose items inside were exactly the treasure that she was looking for.

"Mrow?" Mack had found his way into the room and was staring quizzically at the woman on the floor. Mack liked her, she smelled right, and she had a warm lap. He knew if he looked at her long enough, she'd call his name and he could lie in that lap again.

"Hey Mack. What's the matter, baby? Come sit with me." The tabby rested his head on Kris' arm and closed his eyes. Kris could feel the vibration of his contented purring through the sleeve of her flannel nightgown. She carefully turned pages and moved clippings and other loose papers, learning volumes as she read. There were death notices for Mel ranging from the local paper to one pulled from a national magazine, but on each of them, Keith had scrawled "my fault". There were photos of a Keith that Kris hadn't met; a beaming, happy man with his arms around a woman that her clearly adored. A single portrait, however, made her gasp. It was Mel, looking out of the frame, most likely at Keith, with a smile so gorgeous and loving that it made Kris cry. She sobbed, her body heaving but she made no sound, hoping to not disturb anyone else in the home. She was supposed to find this, she thought, and she was sure that Mel made it happen. All the threads had finally come together, but the knots created were affecting them all.

"Oh my God, Lannie... where did you learn to do that?"

"As I said, putty in my hands, Boo-Boo." The two of them were still on the couch, Boo reclined and Lannie with his foot in her hand. The two bottles had grown to six, and they were both pleasantly drunk. "You have to take a certain number of electives in college, y'know? Well, I took a semester of Holistic Medicine and acupressure was one of the things that I learned. Better than sex, right?" Lannie giggled. She realized that she was letting the beer make her a little, no, a lot looser than she'd been since Boo arrived, but she didn't mind. They'd talked a lot in the last hour or two, and when Boo let his erudite façade down, Lannie had found a lot to like. He'd come to grips with that fact that he'd chased a mirage all the way to this cabin, and admitted that it was a dumb decision in the first place. He was still very cute, and he had the shoulders of a ditch digger, all hard muscle and coiled strength. Lannie had to work with her elbows in order to get those damn things to relax. "You're a grad student and an amateur book reviewer, how did you get built like this?" She'd asked. Swimming was the answer, breaststroke, specifically. He had a buddy on the swim team that let him in the side door during practices and he swam laps in the diving pool until the divers would arrive. Lannie learned a few other things while Boo rambled. He had a good family, good friends, and a solid, if not ambitious, outlook on life. In turn, Boo heard about Lannie's destructive ex, her proclivity for hopeless causes, and even talked her into singing "I Feel Pretty". They laughed together, easily, and the room seemed to swell, soaking up something that hadn't been present in a long time.

"I'm still in school really to avoid the workaday world, Lannie. That, and to flirt with young girls. You don't realize how old twenty-five feels sometimes." Lannie received that reply when she was trying to figure Boo's age by asking why he was a grad student. They had come to the conclusions that Boo was looking for a jolt to put him on the path toward the rest of his life, and that Lannie hadn't really fallen in love with Keith, she was simply trying to save yet another human being, albeit this one was someone that she truly cared about.

"Here and now..." Lannie mumbled. Boo took his foot back and straightened. He was down to just his jeans, due to the massage, and Lannie had put on his flannel, as the fire needed another log. He looked a little closer at Lannie and realized that her sweater was on the floor, and that his shirt was her only cover against the cooling air of the room.

"Hmm, I don't remember that coming off, where was I?

"In front of me. Your damn shoulders were so tight that I worked up a sweat. So, off it came." She crossed her arms. A little self-consciousness invaded her face, and Boo inched closer.

"I'll put some more wood in the fireplace, if you want..." he offered, hoping that his warmth would be preferable to her. "It really is quite tragic, you know. All of this. I feel sorry for Keith, I really do, but, God, shouldn't he have stopped mourning by now?" Lannie nodded. "I agree, but he's the one who has to find the way. It would kill Mel, no pun intended, to see him this way. It kills me." She moved a bit closer to Boo, needing to share his space.

"Maybe something can be done in the morning, but there's nothing to be done tonight." He ran his fingers through Lannie's hair, and she put her head on his shoulder. "You know, my plan was to follow a woman here and then fall in love. Maybe it was a good plan, and I just had the wrong woman in mind." Lannie smiled up at him, and then slowly, deliberately kissed his neck and throat. She pushed herself up with a hand on Boo's chest and with a devilish look in her eye, carefully removed the flannel and her bra, dropping both to the floor. She wrapped her arms around him and pulled in close, cooing ever so slightly as she felt his heat and breathed in the luscious smell of his skin. It had been too long since she'd felt this right, this close to anyone.

"Then I'll have to make sure that you keep me there."

Of course Keith couldn't sleep. He was tired, but his mind raced and ran circles. The rain had stopped and that had allowed him to hear beer bottles clinking together and music playing low simply added to the fodder. He'd never pictured Lannie as being anything but professional, and certainly not easy, but something was going on in the living room that his imagination couldn't let go. He hoped to God that no one was having sex on his couch. He'd burn the fucking thing before he'd sit on it again. How did recent events conspire to screw up his life so? All he wanted to do was write his awful books and be left alone. Why couldn't anybody understand that? *Because you don't understand it.* It was Mel's voice in his head again, and she was right. It was just easier to be alone. Not better, and not what he really wanted, but easy. He'd mourned for so long, but had never truly accepted her being gone. Denial and ignorance were his shields, and they had worked, until today. Until Lannie, and Boo, and Kris. Keith sat up, rubbed his eyes and his scalp. Why did he keep thinking about Kris? He felt awful- a first- about how off and on nasty he'd been to her and that was partly why he'd made her promise not to leave tonight. The same applied to the others. Lannie cared about him, he knew, and was only trying to pull him out of his abyss. Boone Arloe, poor Boo, full of grand ideas and cockeyed optimism had simply gotten in over his head, although it seemed that maybe he had found some of what he came looking for, at least by the possible actions down the hall. Keith's confusion over Kris, however, was deeper than a well. "In my arms…" he repeated, quietly. Why had he thought that? Wasn't that a betrayal, treason of the highest order against what he and Mel had built? Or was he allowing himself to let go, even a little bit, of the self-hate in which he was wallowing? Kris made him think about and feel things that he hadn't; she made him expose things to the light of day, and it was liberating. He hadn't been able to think of Mel in this way for a long time and it hurt, but it was a good hurt and he wanted more.

Fourteen

"*K*ris. Kris, wake up, please." An early autumn morning in the North still provides quite a bit of light upon sunrise, and Kris had covered her head with the comforter in an effort to shut out the rays. Keith was gently, probably too gently trying to rouse her, and she was having no part of it. "Fine. The hard way then." He produced a small ball from his pocket and placed it on Kris' quilt-covered head. "Mack, get the ball!"

"Rowl!" said the tabby, as he landed with all fours directly on Kris.

"Ahh! Jesus, I'm up, I'm up..." She shot a dirty look toward Mack, and then continued up to Keith. Bundling the comforter around her and hiding the yearbook that she'd fallen asleep with, she swung her legs out to the floor. "God... is it still dark?"

"Just after sunrise, perfect time for a brisk walk around the property." Keith extended his hand, but it was waved away. He had a somewhat serene look on his face, as if a great calm had settled there during the night. "Did you sleep well? I have to admit, so much time has passed since I've been in that bed, I can't remember how comfortable it is or isn't." Kris lost her irritation and instead was confused. What was going on? Last thing she knew, Keith wanted her gone, and as quickly as possible. She shook out her hair, and stood up, unsteadily. She looked around the room, searching for something.

"Bathroom?"

"No, m' bag. Gotta brush... teeth." She was waking slowly, but Kris had enough of her faculties to realize that acting groggy was her best bet to buy some time. She walked toward the bathroom, noticing that Keith had found her duffle and was holding her brushing supplies.

"Here's what you need. They were on top, so please don't think that I was going through your things." Keith said, honestly hoping that Kris wouldn't feel that way. Kris managed a weary smile and took the brush and toothpaste from Keith's hand. If you only knew what I did last night, buddy, she thought. Still wrapped in the quilt and clutching the purloined yearbook, she shuffled into the bath and locked the door behind her. Once inside, Kris immediately began looking for a hiding place for the book. Keith was being cordial, pleasant even, and she didn't want to risk a blow-up right now. She settled upon stuffing it behind a stack of towels in the linen cubby, and went about brushing her teeth.

"Everything okay? Do you need anything, Kris?" Keith was sitting on the bed, absent-mindedly petting Mack and trying to remember when he had last spent more than a minute or two in this room. The French Country décor hadn't changed since Mel died. Keith changed the sheets, and he dusted and vacuumed, of course, but anything more than that was unbearable; it actually frightened him to be alone in there. This morning, though, it didn't. He'd decided while trying to fall asleep there was something he wanted Kris to see. Him. He wanted her to see the Keith that Mel saw, even if it killed him.

"No, I'm... fine. Be out in second." Kris wiped her mouth and stared at her reflection. She'd read and re-read everything that she found between the covers of the yearbook, and coupled with the novel that started this whole goddamn mess, she had formed a pretty solid picture of who Keith was, and she was starting to care about him. A lot. She looked up at the bathroom windows, tracing the thin beams of red and gold easing up the opposite wall. "Everything happens for a reason, nothing is coincidental." She mumbled.

Keith had always been impatient, even when Mel was alive, so he'd begun to putter around the room while waiting for Kris to exit the bathroom. Into the closet he'd gone, and dug out an old toque and a flannel barn jacket that he thought would make Kris more comfortable on their jaunt. It was funny, but it seemed that the more that he tried to be polite to Kris, the more it was that he thought of Mel, the mundane, everyday type thoughts that nonetheless were warming to his soul. He hadn't felt this good in months, and he was damned well going to enjoy this sudden flush of humanity.

"It looks pretty chilly out there, Keith. I think that it might've even frosted overnight." Kris pulled her hair into a loose ponytail as she headed toward the bed, and she'd exchanged the nightgown for a pair of nicely faded Levi's. She carried the slight pout of a schoolgirl that doesn't want to catch the bus, and placed her hands on her hips, silently asking Keith to reconsider this "walk" stuff.

"I may need to check the furnace, 'cause it seems that it's also a little chilly in here."

"Hmmm?"

"Your headlights, Kris. They're on."

Wide-eyed understanding preceded the gasp, but only by milliseconds. "Oh. My. GOD! Turn around, turn around, Keith! Shit!" Crossing her arms tightly, Kris hurried to her bag and dumped its contents to the floor, grabbing the first bra that she saw. Fittingly, it was as red as her cheeks were becoming. Since all women are members of the Professional Underwear Wearers Union, it took Kris merely an instant to don her garment, and she didn't even need to remove the tee that had been such little protection against the morning chill. Deciding that being a bit "nipply" wasn't the worst thing that could have happened, she took a deep breath and centered herself. "There, no more high-beams. See, it is too cold."

"These will help." Keith held out the hat and coat. "It just happens to be more peaceful this time of the day, and you may see things that you haven't before." He stepped closer, and Kris' arms uncrossed. "You'll be fine. Mel never complained about the cold when she was wearing them." Keith leaned in and pulled the cap down over Kris' head, stopping just before it covered her eyes. The thumb of his left hand lightly brushed her cheek, giving her a slight tingle, but for the first time since her arrival, Kris noticed that Keith still wore his wedding ring, and the sight of that plain, gold band replaced her warm shiver with a dry queasiness in the middle of her gut.

"Are you sure about this, Keith? I mean, Mel's stuff?" She knew that it was the right thing to ask, but it didn't stop her from slipping the jacket over her shoulders. She quickly buttoned it and flipped the collar up to cover her cheeks, and doing so, noticed the faint smell of what must have been Mel's perfume, and the scent centered her.

"You need to be warm, and you'd swim in my extra things, so this is the only viable option." She looks adorable, Keith thought, just like Mel did. More memories flooded Keith's mind; of walks just like on which he and Kris were about to embark, of watching Mel swish her feet in the creek that ran through the land when she was too hot to keep going during summer hikes. Thoughts of picnic dinners and star-lit love-making and of staying up to see the sunrise, and the punchy laughter that always accompanied lack of sleep. Usually, remembering things would cause Keith to crash, and find another bottle to hide in, but today, every thought of his wife buoyed him, brightened him, and made him want to keep seeking her.

"You're grinning. I'm a huge dork, right?" Kris shifted her weight back and forth, trying not to be too impatient or too self-conscious. She wasn't doing very well with either.

"Actually, you look very cute, and the smile is because you made me think about Mel in a good way, not a self-destructive one." Keith glanced at his wrist. "We need to get going. Nature is best appreciated at first light. Oh, and we should hit the trail from back here. I don't think we need to go through the living room to the front door."

Kris caught Keith's shudder as he mentioned the living room, and her interest was piqued. "Why don't we want to go through the living room?"

Keith sighed. "Lannie and Boo are asleep and naked, and I'd rather they wake on their own and explain things to us once they have their stories straight than startle them and avert my eyes from all the bare, embarrassed skin."

Embarrassed? Kris' mind was already there.

"Lannie and Boo? Ewwww!" She stuck out her tongue. "I so do not need that visual in my head."

Keith guided her toward the doors to the deck. "Understood. And remind me to burn that couch, will you?"

Fifteen

The main window of the living room faced the east, in order to let the sun's first rays light and warm the most comfortable room in the home. At this moment, however, a persistent beam was doing its darnedest to wake Lannie. She squinted and yawned, then propped herself up on one elbow, trying to figure out where her watch had gone. A cursory look at the floor revealed the strap peeking out from under her sweater. "Seven-twelve? God, it's early." Lannie fastened the clasp and straightened a little, pulling the sheet from the hideaway over her breasts. She looked to her right, settling on a still-sleeping Boo, and smiled with satisfaction. "My beautiful Boo. What a gentleman you turned out to be." She gently ran her fingers through his hair, trying not to wake him, but needing to touch him, just a little bit. It would have been easy to blame the night's event on the beer, or even spite, but Lannie was determined to tell herself the truth. She slept with Boo because she wanted to. That's it, end of story. She wanted to because of all that they had talked about, and all that they had shared. In Boo, Lannie found someone who was willing to listen and really hear her, and in turn, Lannie treated Boo like an adult, one that had something to offer. He'd mentioned that he'd felt rudderless until reading the book, and that those words had sparked something purposeful inside of him. Lannie told Boo everything that she knew about Keith and Mel, and how Keith had said that he could feel Mel's presence around him while he wrote. She felt that somehow, the story carried Mel's spirit, and that Keith had tapped into a muse that he'd never before. That was the secret; the book made the reader believe not only that a love that fulfilling existed, but also that they could discover one just as wonderful for their own. Lannie smiled as she remembered the feeling of "rightness" when she leaned in to kiss Boo's neck, and how all that followed seemed meant to be.

"Kismet. That's what you're thinking about, isn't it?" Boo was awake and snaking an arm around Lannie's shoulder. "Or fate, destiny, serendipity... whatever. You're wondering why what happened, happened."

"Because I wanted it, wanted you, I guess. I'm not sorry about it, though." Lannie took Boo's hand and pulled his arm tighter around her. It was the truth, and she didn't think that Boo was too broken up about it, either, considering his wandering hand. "Ah-ah. Don't be starting anything." She playfully slapped his fingers.

Boo scooted to the side a bit in order to get a better look at Lannie. The sunrise revealed the honeyed highlights in her hair and the glow in her face, things that he hadn't noticed before. He also saw a grace and a calm in her eyes that was slightly unsettling. This was serious to her, not something to be treated lightly. "I need to ask you something. Where do we go from here?

Lannie wasn't surprised by the query, but she decided to make Boo work harder, and find out what was on his mind. "Kitchen. Breakfast."

"You know what I mean. This. Us." Boo was starting to fumble somewhat. It was adorable for Lannie to watch, and she realized that this was probably the first time that Boo actually had stuck around after a night with someone.

She kept playing the game. "There's an 'us' now? I thought that it was just about great sex with guys like you."

"Lannie!" Boo was now turning red. "Okay, I'm not fooling around here-"

Lannie looked down her nose at him. "Uh-huh..."

"Jesus Christ, I'm trying to be serious! Give me a break, please?" He took his arm back and ran his hands through his hair, grimacing. "Yes, the sex was great, but I'm used to that."

"Don't break your arm."

Boo continued. "I mean, as a guy, I'm used to focusing on the physicality of the act, nothing more. Anybody that I've been with before knew the score going in." He placed a hand on hers. "Last night, I was more interested in the emotional connection. How I felt about you rather than how it felt in you."

Now it was Lannie's turn to blush. "Boo..."

"Let me finish, Lannie, please. If I over-think this, I'll screw it up. Last night, all that I wanted to do was take the sadness from you and make things right." Boo took her hand and entwined his fingers with hers. "To want to be that person feels pretty damn good, and I want us to see what this might lead to, because I don't want to chance losing what I've spent so long looking for." He kissed the back of her hand. "Now, I'm done."

The honesty in Boo's eyes was breathtaking, and Lannie admired the boldness with which he'd made his point. She'd admitted to herself while Boo was speaking that something was happening to her where he was involved, but as exciting as that was, it was also a little scary. Lannie needed to take this opportunity to try to get Boo to think logically. "Good, because I need to say some things." She pulled the sheet tighter, not because she was uncomfortable with their nakedness, but she knew that if one of "the girls" happened to pop out, any attention paid to her words by Boo would be rendered null. "Firstly, I've let a couple other 'Moseses' part the Red Sea, if you get the drift."

"I admit that I did notice that you're a natural redhead."

"Hush. Then there's the age thingy. I'm... older than you."

Boo was grinning at her. "Six years. It's not even a generational gap. You'll have to try harder."

Boo was right. Lannie kept pitching them and he kept slamming them out of the park. Maybe he did take this as seriously as she. "Plus, I'm sure that all your pretty college girls back home swallow a line much easier. Among other things..."

"C'mon, Lannie! You're gorgeous, you've as good a body as an eighteen-year old and more brains than ten of them combined. You have life experience, which is irreplaceable. You're confident enough to call 'bullshit' when you see it, but compassionate enough to try to keep people like Keith from destroying themselves. I know you better after one night than any woman I've ever met, and I know that there are libraries of knowledge about you that I've yet to learn." Boo stroked Lannie's face so lovingly that she felt her eyes water. "Don't be afraid of this."

Lannie leaned in to kiss Boo as a few tears started down her cheeks. "I am afraid. I've failed at this before, more than once. You're asking for a huge leap of faith from me, huge." She kissed him again, and again. Each time their lips touched it seemed to Lannie that she'd known this man forever, and the butterflies in her gut were singing his praise. She drew his hand under the sheet to her breast, and kissed him harder. "If I jump, you can't let me fall. You can't." Lannie then slid her arms around Boo and buried her face in his chest. She wanted this, and she was ready to face the chasm again.

Boo lifted her chin gently. "I won't."

They held each other that way, sitting up in the bed until they both began to giggle about the mutual stomach growling that was occurring below the sheet and blanket. Lannie gave Boo a devilish glance. "I believe that I mentioned breakfast earlier, didn't I?"

"You did. Do you cook?"

"T-n-N, Boo Boo. Thaw and nuke. That's where the culinary skills end." She traced ticklish circles on Boo's chest. "But I have a feeling that you might know your way around a stove. Something last night about a diner in your youth?"

"You do pay attention, don't you? So, how do you like your eggs?"

Sixteen

Northern Michigan had never held much glamour or mystery for Kris. Being a city girl, she'd always felt that it was simply full of slow times and low culture, but walking through the land around the cabin made her witness to a multitude of charms of which she had no idea. Keith had given her a birding book from a work-shed that was a short walk from the back of the home, and charged her with looking up the names of the beautifully colored specimens that flew around them as they trekked. She was nervous at first, thinking that Keith was testing her, but she soon realized that he was only trying to boost her level of interaction with the nature around her.

"Are you tired? We've only a little more to go." Keith paused in the path and looked back at Kris. "You've done a great job with the birds, by the way."

Kris grinned at the compliment, and even blushed a little. In spite of her earlier misgivings, she was enjoying herself, and Keith was right, it was amazing out here. "Thanks, and no, I'm not tired. I'm glad that you grabbed the book, though. I'm learning a lot."

"We can all stand to learn something." Keith turned and re-took the trail. A very long time had passed since he'd traversed these leafy byways, but each step could have been taken with his eyes closed, using only his memories of Mel as his guide. The countryside, the nature, it all was as much of a home to the two of them as the cabin had been. Mel blazed these trails, with Keith following behind, bending saplings and moving rocks, making paths that only the two of them would be able to find. He was pleased that it came back so easily, and realized that he was thinking of Mel yet again without guilt or pain.

"Not to complain, or anything…" Kris started, "but does this hike have a destination, or are you going to walk until I fall down?" She spoke with her head buried in the book, and without noticing that Keith had stopped, barreled directly into his back. She exhaled hard as the book caught her hard on the bridge of her nose, and waved her hand as her eyes moistened.

"Does that actually work? Mel used to do it too, and she'd never answer the question."

"Does what work?" Kris sniffed, running a sleeve under her nose.

"The wave. My guess is 'no', since your eyes are still watery, and your nose is running." Keith gently took Kris' arm and led her to his side. "This is what I thought that you should see." The trail opened to a clearing with a running stream that was currently hosting a white-tailed doe and two fawns. Keith and Kris shuffled quietly to a pair of Adirondacks and sat down. "This was her spot, her sanctuary. She composed many a painting sitting here." He watched the doe bound off with her children close behind. "I haven't been here since she died."

Kris put her hand on his. "I'm sorry. I can see why an artist would love it here; it is breathtaking." Kris was hoping to keep Keith in the moment, and was afraid that his darkness would return, but he surprised her.

"I'm the one who should be sorry. For all my rambling and whining about losing her again, I'm the one who hasn't gone looking for her. I haven't slept in our bed. I haven't re-hung her paintings." He sighed, and leaned forward, taking his hand from Kris and folding it into the other.

"It was an accident, Keith. It wasn't your fault that Mel died."

"Part of me knows that, that it was just tragic happenstance, but I also know that she wasn't feeling the best that morning. I could have convinced her to stay home. Hell, I could've just picked her up and thrown her back into bed." He squinted. "You never allow that a simple goodbye could be the last one you ever hear. People just don't think like that."

"Why should we, really?" Kris watched a wistfulness wash over Keith's face as he measured her words. "Look, where does fatalism get anyone? All it does is allow you to overlook what's right in front of you." Kris punched Keith in the shoulder to punctuate her statement. She knew that this was her chance to finally reach Keith, to take his hand and pull him away from his own darkness. He seemed to be ready to take that step, and selfishly, Kris wanted to be the one that took it with him. "All of this…" she started as she opened her arms toward the clearing and stood, "wouldn't be yours if not for Mel. Nor would you have had your writing career, and therefore no book to act as a love letter to her." Kris turned to Keith and held out her hand. "Anyone that reads that book will feel what you felt for Mel, and how great a love can be. Isn't that the best way to memorialize her?"

Keith squeezed her hand and sighed. Everything that Kris said made sense, but it was hard to accept. He'd put so much effort into his self-centeredness, so much care into becoming all the worst that he had to offer that he was afraid to step out of his box. He gazed toward the cabin. Boo, Lannie and Kris all ended up on his doorstep yesterday due to a fearlessness of spirit and a need to chase a dream, and they all were inspired by reading the words dedicated to Mel. They had listened to her voice, and it was high time for Keith to do the same.

"He knows food, I'll give him that..." Boo was happily digging through the pantry while Lannie was slicing homemade bread into thick slabs of crusty, yeasty heaven. Boo closed the door with his foot as he wheeled toward the island with an armload of treats. He'd decided that he would make stuffed French toast for Lannie, and had seen her eyes dance at the thought. He put down his load on the opposite side of the island from her and began his work. Lannie watched him carefully fold the apricot butter into the marscapone cheese, and remembered how deftly his hands had worked on her only hours before.

"Do you think that he saw us?"

"Who, Keith?" Boo answered, not raising his eyes from the mixing bowl. "Most likely. I heard him grumbling as he walked past." Satisfied with the texture of the filling, he looked Lannie in the eye, then leaned in and kissed her forehead. "Does it matter?"

Blushing slightly, Lannie grinned toward the floor. "It shouldn't, and I guess that I may be being silly, but I don't want him thinking that I do this all the time."

"Do what? Screw younger men for food?"

"Smart-ass. Keep it up and you'll be wearing that cheese." She didn't stop smiling as she chided Boo, though. She beat milk and eggs into froth, stopping only to allow Boo to add vanilla and cinnamon to the wash. Last night had been amazing, Lannie thought. Never before had she had someone understand her the way that Boo did, and no one had been as truthful, either. She pulled the collar of the purloined flannel that she was still wearing around her face, savoring the scent of the man to which it belonged. She picked up her coffee and glided to the table. "I've done my part, and the griddle's hot, ace."

"It'll be just a minute," Boo said as he grabbed a skillet from the rack above his head. "I saw some sausage and leftover potatoes and onions in the fridge that'll make a killer hash. Besides, I probably should make enough for Kris and Keith, eh?" The cooking was enjoyable to Boo, and the multi-tasking kept him from thinking too much about... everything. Any slight pause, however, and his mind locked in on images of Lannie. Boo was already dreading the trip back home, afraid that the city and its pace would conspire to wreck what he and Lannie had just begun.

"What's the faraway look for, Boo Boo? You didn't chop something off, did you?" Lannie watched him place the finished meat and vegetables into the skillet that he'd dressed with bacon fat. She thought that she'd better re-up her gym membership if he were to cook like this all the time.

"No, just... thinking. How are we going to do this, once we get away from here?"

"I do have a kitchen, you know." Lannie laughed as she ducked the towel that came flying her way.

"Seriously. I'm scared that this will be some type of 'summer camp' romance."

Lannie turned in her chair to face Boo. "Is that what you want it to be?"

"No."

186

"And neither do I. I've had flings; hate 'em." Lannie walked over and put her arms around Boo's shoulders. "I'm also getting tired of repeating myself. I want this to happen. I want us to try to make this work. Why do you keep worrying and second-guessing how I feel?" She emphasized her question with a soft breath in Boo's ear and a kiss to his neck.

"I'm gonna cut something off if you don't cut that out." Boo put the knife in the sink, and turned to face the beauty that was again raising his blood pressure. He saw the trust that she mentioned in her eyes, along with an evenness that wasn't there when he'd first met her. The truth was that he was afraid of letting her down, afraid of hurting her, but he was just as ecstatic that this thing between them was progressing so quickly. Boo was himself around Lannie from the get-go. He'd tried to put on airs for Kris, but had had no desire at all to do the same for Lannie. He could feel the search that she'd been on; it mirrored his own. He instantly wanted to be her best friend as they talked last night, and the love-making wasn't forced, but a natural progression. Suddenly, he knew that the angel and the devil on his shoulders were in agreement: "Why ask why?" So he stopped.

"You're thinking. I can tell by the furrow in your forehead." Lannie playfully flicked a finger at the offending frown.

"Actually, I've stopped. You're right. There's no reason for me to question this. 'Love finds its home…', at least that's what it said in the book that started this whole adventure, right?"

"Um-hmm…" Lannie kissed Boo again. "You couldn't come up with an odder couple than Keith and Mel, yet they were made for each other." She tried to kiss him again, but he held her back slightly. "What?"

"As much as I enjoy the taste of your lips, I'm not going to burn all this food. We can pick this up…"

The end of Boo's sentence was cut off by the slam of a screen door, and the accompanying voice of the cabin owner. "That's probably the most sensible thing that I've heard you say, Mr. Arloe. Let me get my jacket off and I'll set the table for four. I'm famished, and I'm sure that my other guest will be as soon as she finishes her call." The stunned looks on both of their faces filled

Keith with glee. "You also may want to put your shirt back on, too, as food when frying tends to spatter, and grease burns hurt like Hell."

Lannie was glad that she had thrown her tank on under Boo's flannel. Sure, she was still braless, but at least she wasn't topless. It was bad enough knowing that Keith had seen the two of them in bed, so she certainly couldn't bear to have him see her in the buff, at least from her waist to her neck. She handed the shirt to Boo, who wasted no time donning it. "What the heck's gotten into you? You seem positively human." Lannie took a step away from Boo, and instantly cursed herself for doing so.

Keith smiled as he hung his coat. "A good night's sleep unencumbered by alcohol, and a morning walk with a good person. It's a recipe for awareness, I tell you." He continued to smile, ignoring the puzzled looks on the faces of the new lovers, and brought beautiful stoneware out from a tall cabinet. He placed the fourth plate and looked at the two of them. "I've realized that you're all here for the same reason that I am: Melanie. She brought me here, and my memories of her brought you here. I can't disrespect that any longer." Another smile, a thoughtful one this time, bloomed on Keith's face. "I need to make things up to her, and to me, and I need to start now."

Seventeen

*A*t first she was going to text Donna, pretending that she hadn't seen all twelve of the messages that she'd left on Kris' cell. That was a heavy load of avoidance, and Kris thought it would be better to face the music, so she dialed Donna's office. She hung the borrowed coat and hat on hooks in the mud room as the phone rang, and wondered what exactly she was going to tell her friend; hell, she wasn't quite sure what she believed about the whole affair, let alone how to explain it to someone who wasn't there.

"Hello, Bartlett and Associates, Donna D'Andrione speaking…"

"Hey Donna, it's me. Sorry…"

"Me? Who's me? Certainly not my best friend, who went on a desperate adventure and was going to keep me informed of all events in said endeavor."

"Shit, I hate when she plays the victim." Kris thought. "Okay Donna, I'm sorry. I'm sure that you were worried, but things were moving so fast and so oddly that this is the first chance that I've had to call you."

"Um-hm. Well, spill, and I'll see if the story is good enough for me to forgive you."

Kris gave Donna all the info that she felt that she had a right to tell, leaving out a few details here and there out of a sense of privacy to those involved. Silence, which was extremely odd for Donna, was the response. "Do I pass, oh dearest friend of mine?"

"With flying colors, honey. Wow, that could be a book on its own, y'know? By the way, I'm sorry for sending Boo after you. I was just swept up by the romantic bullshit that he was shoveling and I guess that I wanted him to sweep you off of your feet."

"No apology needed, Don. Besides, I think that he may have found what he was looking for, anyway."

"Good for him… and thank you for the call. I should get back to work, and I promise that I won't bother you until you get home, okay?"

"Okay. Love you, bye." Kris folded the phone and placed it in the back pocket of her jeans. She sat down on the bench and took a deep breath. Now came the tough part; going back inside and facing the other three. It was like they'd all been replaced overnight, and the dorkier part of her psyche was half-expecting a pod person of her very own waiting at the table for her. It didn't take a genius to figure out what Boo and Lannie had been up to, but what had gotten them to that point? And Keith? His behavior so far this morning had been enough to make her head swim. Not that she minded, of course. It was nice to not walk on eggshells when he was near, and his company on their walk was quite comfortable. She thought about the goose bumps that had risen with the brush of his hand, and this time there wasn't an accompanying rush of guilt over the desire to feel those bumps again. Even he had admitted that he'd been doing Mel's memory a disservice by acting and carrying on the way that he had, and their conversation at the clearing was most definitely a reach out to Kris. The more that she thought about it, the closer she wanted to get to Keith; to be a friend, a confidant and truthfully, maybe more. What had she started looking for when she left the city a day ago? Finding the source of a love that made her weep in its depth and sweetness was her goal. And what had she found? A curmudgeon who had no idea that in order to memorialize that love he needed to send it out into the world and allow it to come back to him.

Kris sighed, and the escaping breath took with it the doubt that was trying to sink its hooks into her psyche. In high school and in college, boys had come and gone, none really mattering enough to break her heart, and her post-graduation life had been more about finding her path than searching out a soul mate. This was new, uncharted territory, and she'd been drawn here just as the morning sun had drawn the songbirds. Kris' beliefs allowed her that everything happens for a reason, and that the dearly departed can affect the waking world. Just as you can't deceive the dead, you also can't betray them, as long as you don't betray yourself. Kris had finally realized that her purpose was to break Keith's cycle of self-destruction. She had to make him feel for someone else again. If in doing so she found the companion that she was supposed to find, then that was just the icing on the proverbial cake. Fate, kismet or God's will, something had set all of this in motion, and it was time for Kris to open herself to it fully, without armor, and let the pieces fall where they may.

Eighteen

A slightly sarcastic yet still endearing cheer came up from the table as Kris walked into the kitchen, following her nose to the welcoming repast that Boo had prepared. Tucking into a steamy plate of French toast, Kris hadn't been aware of how hungry her nature walk with Keith had made her. She also didn't notice the mixture of maple and marscapone that was dribbling down her chin, until Keith reached over and gently swiped it with his napkin. Sheepishly, she thanked him and returned his smile, thankful that no one else could see those damned goose bumps that he'd given her once more. Anxious to move the spotlight, she addressed the chef.

"This is wonderful, Boo. So, what's up with you and Lannie?" No sooner had she finished her question that it was her turn to offer a napkin; this time to Keith, who'd nearly choked on a bite of hash. As he drew it from her fingers, Kris felt the back of her knees sweat, and she really hoped that she wasn't blushing, but damn, had it gotten warmer in here?

"You should give a warning before you're going to be blunt, you know. I expect it from myself, but not from you." Keith wadded the napkin and handed a clean one back to Kris. "But since the subject's been raised, do tell you two, how did you come to be naked, together, on my couch?"

Boo looked at Lannie and swallowed hard. He had no idea where to start, and judging by the consternation on Lannie's face, neither did she. How would you explain it? At least, how would you without making it sound entirely too lurid and cheap? Boo opened his mouth, still not sure what he meant to have come out, and croaked, "Huh?"

Lannie, per her nature, leapt to his rescue. "This is going to sound stupidly cliché, but one thing led to another, and the end result was what you both saw."

"Not me, just Keith. And he told me to remind him to go shopping for a new sofa." Kris nudged Keith's foot and was greeted with a stern indifference. At least the cold shoulder got rid of her knee sweats.

Keith sighed. "Go on, Lannie."

Lannie looked at her plate, then at Boo, who smiled wanly and squeezed her hand. "I was feeling sorry for myself and Boo called me on the carpet for it. All of this started with the idea that I could use Kris' discovery to worm my way into more of a relationship with Keith than what I had, and..."

"Lannie! Ixnay on the is-kray!"

"He already knows, Kris. I told him last night, but he'd surmised it on his own." Lannie leaned in and kissed Boo's cheek.

The peck settled Boo's nerves enough that he was able to take over, and he did, after one more gulp of milk. "Lannie let Kris follow her here hoping to shake Keith up enough to re-open his heart. I came here hoping to convince Kaycee – er, Kris - , to fall for me. I was feeling as much an idiot as Lannie, and we all know that misery loves company."

Kris was still mystified. "But to hook up after... an afternoon?"

Lannie grinned. "You've no idea how long I've been looking for something, or someone. If Keith has paid any attention to the things that I've said to him over the last four years, he'd agree that my life's been mostly empty since my break-up."

"I wouldn't have said 'empty', unfulfilled, maybe..."

"Also frustrated. I needed someone to save and I thought, or hoped, that Keith would be the one to love me for it."

"I'm sorry...?"

Lannie waved him off and shrugged. "Don't be. I'd spent so much time doing things for others that I didn't realize that I needed to save myself." Lannie was prepared to feel embarrassed after she finished, but instead she felt good, proud even, to have expressed what she'd needed to admit for so long.

"We all needed it, Lannie. Saved from what we were leading ourselves into becoming. You were the saint, Kris was the virgin. Keith, the cynic, and me as the intellectual. All of us eschewing love, true love, as something best left to others." Boo sat up a bit straighter, as if to give his statement more heft, but it was an unnecessary gesture as a quick pass around the table revealed faces full of recognition.

Before the silence became uncomfortable, Kris spoke. "The virgin, eh?"

Boo smiled. "Sure, in the literary sense. Lannie said that you had never been in a serious relationship." He grabbed a stray bite of sausage from his plate and chewed as he finished his thought. "I think that's why you fell into the book so deeply." Boo pulled Lannie's chair closer, and she put a hand on his shoulder. He turned and kissed her, but caught himself before he began to ignore the others. Greeted with a roll of the eyes from Keith and a frown from Kris, he ran a hand through his hair and sighed. He'd never been in love with anyone before, but there was something so right about Lannie, and even though he'd voiced his concerns about the magic disappearing once they got back to "real life", his gut kept telling him not to worry. "Last night, while Lannie and I were talking about... everything, in the back of my mind I was trying desperately to define what was happening. Then she got out of bed, and as beautiful a sight as it was to watch her glide to the kitchen while lit by the flames in the fireplace, my immediate reaction was that I wanted her back next to me. In thirty seconds, I missed her."

"You mean you were still horny..."

"Asshole!" Kris slapped Keith on the back of his head and glared at him when he turned to face her. "How about giving someone the benefit of the doubt for once? You were saying, Boo?"

Lannie mouthed a "thanks" and then took over the story. "*I* was still horny, if that counts. There might be something to that sexual peak thing that I keep reading about, but I digress. We'd already made an emotional connection before anybody's clothes came off, and the lovemaking was the next logical step. I haven't felt as free with myself, emotionally or physically, as I had last night in years. No pun intended, but in just a few hours

Boo managed to fill every hole that I'd been neglecting, and I'd be lying if I said that I wasn't falling for him." Lannie had tears in her eyes, but the most beatific look on her face that she could manage. She knew as well as she knew her name that every moment of her life had led her to be in this cabin at this very time to meet this very man. She'd found what she deserved, finally.

Nineteen

*K*ris volunteered Keith and her to clear the table and wash the dishes so that Boo and Lannie might get on the road quicker. Mack happily ignored everyone in order to clean a few plates on his own, then retreated to the living room to waste a few hours in the warm sun. Boo had a deadline for the University press, and Lannie had no intention of sticking around if Boo wasn't going to be there. The two of them had decided, with a little input from the other pair that they wouldn't move in with each other right away, and that they would take things as maturely as they possibly could. Once the happy couple was out of earshot, Keith confided with Kris that he was still skeptical of Boo, but that he was excited for Lannie and regretted all the nastiness that he'd given her. The main thing that continued to bother him was the admittance of hoping that something would have developed between the two of them.

"Why would she want to pursue anything with me, Kris? I don't get it. Truthfully, I was an ass in the beginning, yet she kept coming back up here." He pulled up his sleeve with his chin in order to keep it out of the dishwater. "Lannie was the first person to be in this house besides me after Mel died. I guess in a way she started pulling me back into the world." Staring off through the window over the sink, he nearly missed the hand-off of a clean plate to Kris, who also seemed lost in thought. He opened his mouth to continue, but was interrupted by one of his fleeing guests.

"Hey you." Lannie set her purse down and pulled Keith's shirt to turn him around. He wiped the suds away on his shirt tail and smiled. Lannie took his hands in hers and stood on her toes to give Keith a kiss goodbye. He was surprised by the gentleness of her gesture, and was taken aback as he realized that he hadn't kissed (or been kissed by) anyone since Mel had died. He wondered how he'd ever let himself disengage from the life that he and his wife had created, and how he'd willfully ignored all of the reminders of a woman that he'd loved more than life itself. "I didn't mean to make you blush, Keith. Did I do something wrong?"

Keith backed away, but only slightly. "It's nothing, Lannie. It's just… I took a full year and a lot of booze to turn into a jackass, and I'm trying to look at things differently now. You reminded me that I hadn't had a kiss in a very long time." It was Lannie's turn to blush now, and she dipped her gaze in order to look at anything other than Keith's face. "Lannie, its nothing. I have to push through this sort of situation, instead of yelling at someone and grabbing a drink. You need to quit worrying about me and take stock in yourself." He lifted her chin and motioned toward the door, where Boo was waiting. "I honestly don't know what you've found in him to fall in love with, but I do believe in your judgment of character. I hope that you can be happy with him, but I hope that you'll finally be happier with yourself."

Lannie beamed at Keith, and hugged him again. She was no longer worried about him drinking himself to death, nor was she afraid that she'd made a wrong turn in entering this relationship with Boo. For the first time in a long time, she was comfortable with who she was and her place in the universe. Finally, she'd made a choice that was right for her, and she'd be damned if she wasn't going to follow it through to the end. "I'll be fine, Keith. You've got to tend to yourself as well. I see a different guy right now, and maybe he's not quite the one that Mel loved, but he's better than the alternative. You gave me and a couple of strangers a chance here, now give yourself one." She uncoiled her arms from Keith's waist and walked quickly to the door. She stopped halfway to whisper something to Kris, kissed her on the cheek, and continued to Boo's side. As the couple left, Lannie yelled. "I'm counting on you… both!"

"She's excited. I'm happy for her." Kris closed the door and joined Keith in the living room. Seconds after she sat down, a furry blur leapt into her lap and began to purr like no feline had ever purred before. She scratched behind his ears and Mack got even louder. "I guess that makes two of us, hey buddy?" She looked up at Keith, whose wry smile she couldn't read. Sitting no more than five feet in front of her, he wore the look of the sage that knows more than anyone else. Quickly, Kris tried to recall anything that Keith might be holding over her, and suddenly, she was struck: she'd forgotten about the...

"So you found the trunk in the closet?"

"How did you...?"

"When I got back inside ahead of you, I ran upstairs to quickly wash my hands. I grabbed a fresh towel from the shelf without looking, and heard a clunk. I know that I possess meager laundry skills, but even I'm aware that they're not supposed to make that much noise. At least clean ones aren't. Imagine my surprise when I turn and find a yearbook half hiding behind the last towel." Keith reached behind the chair and produced the ragged item. He held it out toward Kris. "Was it as good a read as the novel?"

Kris twisted in her seat and her heart sank. Not only was she angry with herself for not putting the book back in the trunk, but she despaired that all of the progress that Keith had seemed to make was lost. "Keith, please don't be mad. I just stumbled upon the trunk, and…"

"I'm not angry. Truly, I'm not." His smile had left, but his eyes were still warm, and newly wistful. "Did you gain any insight? Perhaps something that I might have missed?" His voice was pleading, hoping that Kris really had discovered something that Keith had long put aside or ignored completely. If she couldn't help, then he feared that the man that he'd shared with Mel was gone for good.

Kris swallowed hard, stalling in order to find the right words. This was it, her moment to take the stand that needed to be taken. It was now up to her, alone. "Why do you blame yourself? It was a horrible accident that took Mel, but an accident nonetheless.

Sure, it's awful and shitty and unfair, but you had nothing to do with it!" Her voice had risen, riding the emotions that were cresting in her mind, and Mack jumped down from her lap, hoping that he wasn't the cause. She kept going. "I read the letters that you had collected in that trunk. There were notes from her brother and from her parents; from her friends and acquaintances. Even a guy that she dated in high school jotted down a few lines, and every one of them says the same thing. They all wrote to tell you that no matter how hard it would be to go on, it was the only thing that Mel would've wanted you to do." Kris scooted closer to Keith and put her hand on his knee. She took a deep breath, and kept going. "They also wanted you to know that she felt that you were the best thing that ever happened to her. She told everyone that no man could ever have loved her as much as you did and that she'd never felt more complete than when she'd said to you, 'I do'."

"I didn't put a lot of weight into what those letters contained, I guess because I felt that they just wanted to say the right things." He sighed deeply and looked past

Kris, trying focus his mind. To hear Kris' view of his past was to see himself from outside the box, and to see what maybe his wife had seen in him as well.

Kris knew that she needed to keep pushing. "They did say the right things, because it was the truth. These were people who loved and respected Mel, and they wouldn't sully her memory by lying to you. They wanted to help. You wouldn't let them. You wouldn't blame the poor man that caused the accident, and you couldn't blame God, so you picked yourself to bear this cross. The problem is that you didn't work through the pain and loss, but you latched onto self-pity and misery instead. You hid in a bottle in order to avoid closure, but what you really did was ignore the love and the memories that were surrounding you; the very things that would've made you feel closer to Mel even though she wasn't there."

Kris opened the book and handed him the portrait. "She didn't die because of you Keith, but if she doesn't live on, it will be on your hands." She rubbed her teary eyes with her sleeve and sniffled. "My God, but I'm sick of crying. I've left enough water here to take care of your lawn." Kris cleared her throat and steeled for one final salvo. "Keith, you need to make this choice, right now. I've never felt in my life the kind of love that you had, but I want to, and… I want to with you. I want to be the one that pulls you through this. I want to know you the way that Mel did. I can't… I *wouldn't* want to replace her, but let me fall in love with you."

Keith stared at Kris, then down at the portrait. "Just to see her smile made me happy, you know? If Mel was happy, so was I. It's silly, but it was that simple." He looked around the room and smiled. Was it really though? Had he just discovered the key under the doormat after all this time? "I loved her… no, I love her so much."

"I know."

"I see a lot of her in you, though."

"Flatterer. I'm not that strong."

Keith shook his head. "Don't sell yourself short. It takes a lot of guts to put up with what you have in this house and still want my company." He gathered his thoughts while Mack did a figure-eight around his legs and then jumped into Kris' lap once again. "Then there's the fact that Mack adores you."

Kris rubbed the tabby's ears. "How could he not, right Mack?"

"How could he not, indeed. I meant what I said. Do you really think that I'd have allowed just anyone to sleep in that room, or wear those clothes? When I woke you this morning, I felt something that I haven't in a long time. I felt anticipation… and hope. I was anxious to get going and to show you what was outside; my world, so to speak. I told the others before you came in that I'd had an epiphany, and I do believe that I have." He gathered himself, emotionally *and* physically, and crossed the small distance between them. Kneeling in front of Kris, he found her eyes. The width and depth of them revealed to Keith that he was right in deciding to take this new path; Kris was welcoming his presence, whether or not she realized it. After a deep breath, Keith continued. "Writing the book gave me the means to re-connect with Mel, and I squandered that. Seeing first hand how that story affected all of you has given me another chance. It's a chance that is probably my last. I've been alone too long Kris and this loneliness may kill me if I don't change now. I want to be the man that I was when Mel was alive, and I'm asking you to help me get there."

Twenty

A couple of hastily packed bags sat near the door of the cabin, and a very curious tabby was trying to open the duffle by way of knocking off the handles. Since that wasn't working, he decided to saunter toward the voices that he was hearing and involve himself in whatever was happening in the dining room.

The weekend had passed and the rays of a Monday morning sun were warming the cabin to a point of almost unbearable coziness. Mack had entered the room where the voices of both his oldest friend and his newest were emanating, and plopped down in the middle of the brightest patch of sun to listen.

"You've got everything packed? I'll put your bags in the car if you'd like."

Kris grinned, but shook her head. "I can handle it. Besides, you're trying too hard. When we agreed that I'd stay here for the rest of the weekend, we also said that we'd let this play out on its own terms. You've still got to be yourself. I don't expect Prince Charming."

Keith chuckled, and enjoying the sound of his own laughter, smiled broadly. "Right, right. Is it okay to say that I'm glad that you stuck around?"

"Of course. I'm glad too. I've told you many times in the last couple of days how much I want this, but I won't cheapen it by pushing either of us into something that doesn't fit." Kris hugged Keith tightly, and gave him a light kiss on the cheek. She felt a twinge of sadness as she left his arms, but it was quickly replaced by the exhilaration of new beginnings. She had always loved a challenge, and anything that was worthwhile took hard work. Plus, she wasn't making this trek alone. On her way to the door, she looked back and caught Keith with his arms full of cat. She laughed and thought that this wasn't too bad a place to be, and she would take every chance to be here forever.

~

"What a week, eh Mack?" An affirmative sounding meow was the answer that Keith received while he puttered around the kitchen. The two of them made promises to each other before Kris left: She would be back in about ten days and he would work toward returning all of his memories of Mel to their rightful places. He'd told Kris that he already planned to re-hang Mel's art, and therefore he'd be unable to shirk from that duty knowing the grief he'd get upon Kris' return. He had gotten Kris to agree to one caveat, though; he would put out only one photograph. Keith argued that it wouldn't be fair to Kris to have to be reminded of Mel every time that she was to visit, but he did need something to make it easier to talk to Mel, wherever she might be. Mack wandered off to find a better sunny spot in which to nap, and Keith moved into the living room, looking to check the fireplace. He poked around the flue and realized that his home didn't have the chill to which he had grown accustomed. Shrugging his shoulders and smiling, he sat back in his chair and raised his cup of tea to the portrait on the mantle. "If I didn't know any better, I'd say that you had a hand in all of this, babe." His only response was the smile on the face of a woman truly in love.